12|17

the Alex Cross,
Bennett and Private novels – and
other number one bestsellers includi
and stand-alone thrillers.

James is passionate about encouraging children to read. Inspired by his own son who was a reluctant reader, he also writes a range of books for young readers including the Middle School, I Funny, Treasure Hunters, House of Robots, Confessions and Maximum Ride series. James has donated millions in grants to independent bookshops and he has been the most borrowed author in UK libraries for the past ten years in a row. He lives in Florida with his wife and son.

BOOK**SHOTS**

STORIES AT THE SPEED OF LIFE

What you are holding in your hands right now is no ordinary book, it's a BookShot.

BookShots are page-turning stories by James Patterson and other writers that can be read in one sitting.

Each and every one is fast-paced, 100% story-driven; a shot of pure entertainment guaranteed to satisfy.

Available as new, compact paperbacks, ebooks and audio, everywhere books are sold.

BookShots – the ultimate form of storytelling. From the ultimate storyteller.

ABSOLUTE ZERO

JAMES PATTERSON

WITH ED CHATTERTON

BOOK**SHOTS**

1 3 5 7 9 10 8 6 4 2

BookShots
20 Vauxhall Bridge Road
London SW1V 2SA

BookShots is part of the Penguin Random House group of companies
whose addresses can be found at global.penguinrandomhouse.com

Penguin
Random House
UK

Copyright © James Patterson 2017

The BookShots name and logo are a trademark of JBP Business, LLC.

James Patterson has asserted his right to be identified as the
author of this Work in accordance with the Copyright,
Designs and Patents Act 1988

First published by BookShots in 2017

www.penguin.co.uk

A CIP catalogue record for this book is available
from the British Library

ISBN 9781786531780

Typeset in Garamond Premier Pro font 11/15.5 pt by Jouve (UK), Milton Keynes
Printed and bound in Great Britain by Clays Ltd, St Ives Plc

ABSOLUTE ZERO

CHAPTER 1

THURSTON'S BEEN DOWN TOO long. Thanks to the hypersensitive security sonar in place, the use of standard-issue dive gear has been ruled out for this mission. Thurston's operating on lung power alone.

Lieutenant Hardacre, the whites of his eyes flashing against the night camo make-up, glances at Green at the tiller of the RHIB. Green shakes his head and checks his watch.

'Seven minutes twenty. Not looking good, sir.'

Hardacre glances across the water at the black mass of the target vessel. They're less than forty metres from the Karachi Naval Yard perimeter. Their target – Thurston's target – is the *Khan*, a Pakistan Navy Tariq-class frigate whose captain has distinct ISIS leanings. US Intelligence suggests in no uncertain terms that the rogue officer is contemplating a major attack on US assets in the Gulf. Exactly what those assets might be, nobody is too sure. But with the frigate packing as much firepower as it does, no one back at Command is taking any chances. In normal circumstances, a black ops team might make the captain disappear, or a drone disable his ship from the comfort of a bunker in Washington.

But these are not normal circumstances.

Because the captain of the *Khan* is the nephew of an extremely high-ranking and well-connected family. For reasons far too complicated for all but the mandarins at Langley to comprehend, this must look like an internal attack: there can be no traceable links back to the US. Hence the use of an Australian team as the pointy end of a dirty spear. None of Hardacre's team are wearing uniform. This mission is as off the books as it is possible to be. Get caught here and there'll be no trial, no covert handover at a checkpoint in Sinai. It'll be a long dusty trip to some Pakistan Intelligence torture camp and the distinct possibility of starting World War Three. All three men wear cyanide capsules on a chain round their necks and none would hesitate to use them. They've seen the results of concerted torture before.

'Jesus Christ, Thurston,' mutters Hardacre.

Green looks up at his boss. 'Eight minutes ten.'

'He's dead. We've got to cut and r—'

'There!' Green points at a spot of black water some twenty metres away. Hardacre can't see a thing but Green is part owl when it comes to night vision.

They paddle the RHIB towards a flurry of rising silver bubbles and arrive as Thurston's head breaks the surface. He throws open his mouth and sucks down a lungful of air. Hardacre leans over and pulls Thurston aboard.

'All good?' says Hardacre.

Thurston, unable to speak, raises a thumb.

'Go,' says Hardacre.

Silently, Green paddles the RHIB out of the dock, past the Pakistan Naval Academy and out into the main channel. Only when the boat is out of earshot does Green start the muffled engine and head slowly and quietly down towards the Marho Kotri Wildlife Sanctuary, where they have established a camp. After a switch into civilian clothes they'll sink the RHIB in the mangroves and slip into Karachi in a day or two to resume their cover work as liaison officers at the Australian embassy.

They've just turned the first corner when the initial blast comes.

'Nice work, Thurston,' says Lieutenant Hardacre.

Thurston nods. 'Thanks, sir.'

'Nine minutes,' says Green. 'You were down nine fucking minutes, mate!'

'Seemed longer,' says Thurston as the sky erupts behind them.

CHAPTER 2

THEORETICALLY, A TEMPERATURE OF absolute zero is a physical impossibility. But rounding the corner of the Hackney Road and copping the whip of the sleet-streaked wind directly into his face, Cody Thurston is pretty sure he's found it.

Jesus, London in January. It never gets any easier.

Not for a boy brought up in Byron Bay anyway.

Thurston tucks his chin deeper into the cowl of his North Face and conjures up memories of a seemingly endless parade of sun-kissed January days on the Far North Coast of New South Wales.

He checks his watch. Eight o'clock on a dog of a night in Hackney, seven in the morning Down Under. The first surfers will already be in the water at the Pass or down at Tallows. Thurston allows himself a brief moment of wishful thinking before shouldering his gym bag and picking up the pace.

Screw that nostalgia shit. The teenage Cody Thurston who surfed like there was nothing else worth living for is long gone. *This* Cody Thurston is right here, right now. And all he's got to look forward to is another shift at the V and the usual sh—

'Mother*fucker*!'

Thurston feels a sharp pain in the back of his kidneys and looks down to see a young guy in a wheelchair cocking his fist for another punch. Thurston swivels out of the way and gives the guy a slap across the back of the head. Not too hard, but enough to let him know Thurston's there.

'Hittin' a cripple, hey? Nice fuckin' work, man! You smack every disabled person you see?'

Thurston shakes his head. 'Only you, Lenin. Only you.'

Lenin smiles, brushes some sleet off his dreads and swings his chair next to Thurston. 'You goin' the V?'

'Same as every night. How about you?'

'Same as every night, man.' Lenin puts on a spurt. 'Race you!'

Thurston watches him go. 'Fuck you. You *hurt* me.'

'Loser!' shouts Lenin as he turns into the warm yellow light spilling out of the door to the V. The crumbling Victorian bar halfway down the Hackney Road has been Thurston's workplace for almost two years. He lives in a cramped two-room attic shoved up under the leaky roof.

It's home.

CHAPTER 3

'YOU'RE LATE, DICKHEAD. THINK I'm made of fuckin' money, Buster?' Barb cackles, making a sound like a parrot gargling nails.

The owner of the V is in her regular spot, perched precariously on a stool in the corner of the bar on the customer side. Barb Connors must be eighty-five if she's a day but there's still something of the King's Cross hooker about her, and it's not just her filthy mouth. She wears a yellow wig that looks like it would survive a nuclear attack and make-up half an inch thick. Her choice of lipstick, as always, is crimson.

Thurston acknowledges his boss but doesn't say anything. As long as she keeps calling him 'Buster' he's going to keep right on saying zip. Barb watched a documentary about silent movies last year and has been trying to make the Buster Keaton thing stick with Thurston ever since. He's having none of it – as much to annoy Barb as for any objection he has to being called Buster. Ignoring the military-grade laser death stare coming at him from Barb's direction, Thurston flips up the bar lid and hangs his sopping jacket behind the door to the cellar.

'Hey, Janie,' says Thurston to a thin blonde punkette with tattooed cleavage who is placing fresh bottles in a cooler cabinet. Thurston makes a point of staring directly at Janie's chest. 'Evening, girls,' he says and waggles his fingers.

Janie Jones reaches down and casually grabs Thurston's nuts. 'Evening, boys,' she replies and squeezes. Hard.

'Jesus!' gasps Thurston.

Janie releases her grip with a sweet smile, flips Thurston the middle finger and continues her task. On the other side of the bar, Lenin laughs and bumps fists with Janie.

'Man's a Neanderthal, Janie.'

Janie doesn't look up. 'He's Australian. What do you expect?'

'I was being ironic,' says Thurston.

'Well, consider that nut squeeze my ironic reply, OK?' says Janie.

'Fair enough,' says Thurston. 'How's it been tonight?'

Janie stands and looks at Lenin, not quite ready to restore peace with Thurston. 'Usual?'

Lenin is staring at Janie's chest so she snaps her fingers in front of his face twice. 'Hey. Hey. Up here. There's nothing ironic about you, Lenin. Usual?'

'Uh-huh,' says Lenin, his eyes remaining glued to Janie's breasts.

While she pours, Janie turns to answer Thurston's question. 'It's been quiet,' she says, shooting a glance at Barb. 'Kind of.' Barb looks at Janie and then back at Thurston. Something's up.

Thurston slides his plastic cash register ID into place and punches in the code. While Janie pours Lenin's drink she taps Thurston with an elbow and flicks her eyes towards a knot of men near the pool table.

There are four of them, all in suits, all in their thirties: beered-up, red-faced, peaking early. Thurston's seen the sort down here plenty of times before: businessmen coming to the V for a bit of authentic old-London-boozer flavour. Slumming it before the inevitable gentrification takes place. They're loud and look as if they could easily be a bunch of dicks but Thurston can't see what the problem might be. Two local girls are with the group but they look happy enough to be there, if a little bored.

They also look about fourteen years old, but Barb has a liberal approach to the drinking age laws.

Thurston raises his eyebrows in a question to Janie. 'Problem?'

Janie shrugs. 'They haven't been here long. Couple of beers, nothing much. Out-of-towners. Tourists. Probably nothin'.'

'They don't look like fuckin' tourists,' says Lenin. 'I don't like 'em.'

Thurston agrees. Now he's had a chance to study them a little longer the group don't look like tourists.

They look like trouble.

One of them, a guy with cropped hair and a thick black goatee, sees Thurston looking their way. Black Goatee holds Thurston's gaze for a few seconds, smiling without warmth. Thurston looks away. There's never any point getting into a pissing contest with a drunk.

'There's another one,' says Janie. 'You'll see. He's in the bog.'

Two more customers come to the bar and Thurston serves them. Sofi Girsdóttir, the V's chef for tonight's shift, comes up shivering from the cellar carrying a can of cooking oil. She mutters something sweary in Icelandic and pats Thurston on the shoulder before heading back into the kitchen.

Which is when Thurston sees the monster.

CHAPTER 4

THE GUY WHO COMES out of the bathroom, dipping his head under the door frame, is huge. A giant.

Thurston hesitates for a fraction of a second and then resumes pouring drinks.

'Unbelievable, hey?' says Lenin. 'Incredible 'Ulk, innit?'

Thurston shakes his head a fraction and glances again at the big man as he joins the rest of the crew at the pool table. Thurston sees Black Goatee point to the giant's upper lip. The guy wipes something off with a hand the size of Nova Scotia. Black Goatee laughs and says something to another guy in the group.

Janie's right: these fuckers are trouble.

As another evening wears on, the V fills, the noise level rising steadily as the alcohol takes hold. Thurston likes it fine that way. The more noise the better, the busier the better.

Less time to think.

An hour in, Black Goatee rocks up to the bar with another guy. The group have been ordering drinks from Janie so far, so it's the first time Thurston's had any reason to hear them speak.

'Five beers, three double Jack and Cokes, *mate*.' Black Goatee speaks with an American accent and says the word 'mate' in what he imagines is a London accent. He stares at Lenin coldly.

The American voice surprises Thurston.

Black Goatee's skinhead sidekick mutters something under his breath. Thurston can't make it out but hears a Russian accent. They are talking about him, that's clear, but Thurston lets it go. It happens every night.

Thurston completes the order in full Buster Keaton mode. When he asks for the money Black Goatee looks up.

'What's your accent, champ? Scottish?' He hands over a fifty.

Thurston notices a faded tattoo creeping out of the end of his sleeve: an eagle of some kind with German-looking text underneath.

'Aye,' he says, handing over the change but saying nothing else.

Black Goatee frowns, aware he's being punked but unsure exactly how. 'Yeah? Don't sound real Scottish now I hear it again.'

Thurston shrugs. 'Born and bred.' He turns to another customer. In his peripheral vision he sees Black Goatee getting wound up.

Before anything else happens, Sofi pushes open the door to the kitchen.

'Cody,' she says, 'have you—'

As she sees the American on the other side of the bar, Sofi stops dead, the colour draining from her face.

'Hey, lollipop,' says the American. He's smiling.

Sofi Girsdóttir turns without speaking and stumbles her way back into the kitchen.

'Sofi?' says Thurston.

'We got to catch up soon, honeybun,' says Black Goatee to the closed kitchen door. He mimes putting a phone to his ear. 'Call me, y'hear?' He and the Russian crack up.

'Do we have a problem here?' says Thurston. There's an edge to his voice that wasn't there before. The exchange worries him. Thurston knows Sofi well enough: she's feisty, independent, and not the sort to scare easy.

'No,' says Black Goatee. 'No problem, chief. Just one old friend catching up with another in jolly old England.' The guy stares at Thurston for a few seconds before letting the Russian drag him back towards the pool table. Thurston has to fight the urge to leap across the bar and wipe the smug smile from Black Goatee's face.

'Forget it,' says Janie quietly, appearing at Thurston's shoulder. 'But keep an eye on them. They give me the creeps. I'll go and check on Sofi.'

Thurston walks down the bar and takes an order from another customer.

Tonight's going to be a long one.

CHAPTER 5

JANIE WAS RIGHT PREDICTING trouble, but when it comes, it isn't from the direction Thurston was expecting.

Three guys in rugby shirts, who've been drinking heavily all night, get into a political debate with, of all people, Lenin. Things escalate when an enraged Lenin punches one of them in the nuts. The men laugh but the guy who cops one to the balls tips Lenin out of his chair.

Thurston is round the bar before Barb can give him the nod.

'Out,' he says, his voice flat. It's a statement, not an invitation.

'Fuck off, Crocodile Dundee,' says the guy whom Lenin hit. His voice has the plummy English accent Thurston hates.

'Out now,' he says.

'Or what?' says one of the others. 'What, precisely, will you do, *cobber*? Throw another shrimp on the barbie?'

Thurston doesn't reply. Instead he steps forward, pulls a pen from his pocket and jams it tight against the throat of the guy who tipped Lenin from his chair. With his mouth close to the guy's ear, Thurston whispers, 'Apologise. Or you get a second hole in your windpipe.'

The plummy-voiced loudmouth is about to react when he looks at Thurston and sees something in the Australian that keeps him still.

'Get your hands off him, you fucking oik!' One of the other rugger buggers takes a step forward. Thurston stops him with a quick shake of the head.

'The night's over, gents,' says Thurston. He drops his hand to his side but knows he'll have no more trouble. 'Go on, out you go. Nice and quiet.'

'Yeah, fuck off,' hisses Lenin, back in his chair. He singles out one of the group and points a finger. 'Come the revolution, bro, you're going down. Believe it.'

Thurston closes the door of the V behind the troublemakers and returns to the bar.

'A pen?' says Barb, one thickly drawn eyebrow raised to within an inch of her dyed hairline.

'Worked, didn't it?'

Thurston looks towards the pool table and, as he knew he would be, Black Goatee is looking in his direction.

CHAPTER 6

THE ALREADY FERAL ATMOSPHERE in the V curdles further as the night wears on. From what Thurston can see, a blizzard of coke is being snorted in the toilets. One sneeze and there'd be a white-out.

'You want me to do something about this?'

Like everyone at the V, Thurston knows coke is a fact of London life. Mostly, so long as there's no obvious dealing taking place, the cops turn a blind eye to the occasional recreational toot. Tonight, though, the group at the pool table are flat out taking liberties and Barb could find herself shut down so fast it would make her nose bleed. Which, from the look of some of the customers, is also a fate they'll be experiencing soon.

'You better tell them to go.' Barb looks at Thurston. 'You sure about this one, Buster? These guys don't look like they'll take a hint.'

'I don't plan to be subtle,' says Thurston. 'There won't be any hinting.'

He wipes his hands on a cloth and moves towards the bar lid. He's about to go through when he stops, hearing a muffled noise in all the cacophony which, without knowing exactly why, sounds out of place. *Wrong*.

'What is it?' asks Barb.

'Where's Janie?' says Thurston, but he doesn't wait for an answer.

Following some base-level instinct, connecting the dots as he runs – Janie taking a cigarette break; the giant glancing her way as she heads to the back of the pub; a couple of knowing looks between Black Goatee and the Russian – Thurston ducks past the toilets and pushes open a fire door to the alley.

Next to the dumpster, Janie Jones is on her knees. The giant from the troublemakers inside is holding her hair bunched in his massive fist. His other hand is unzipping his flies.

'Private party,' rumbles the giant. 'Fuck off.'

Janie, tears running down her face, moans. She moves her mouth but no words come.

'Shut up, bitch!' growls the giant.

Thurston retreats. 'This isn't my scene, man,' he says, holding up his hands. He turns to go. 'Sorry, Janie.'

'That's right, little man, run along and let the grown-ups play.'

Thurston moves away and then, as the giant turns his attention back to Janie, picks up a length of wood leaning against the dumpster, whirls around and cracks it across the man's windpipe.

If a normal human had received the blow, it would have killed them. Instead, the giant buckles at the knees, his hands clutching his throat. Thurston takes two steps forward and, two-handed, cracks the wood over the man's skull. He falls to the ground, motionless.

Janie Jones gets to her feet and kicks the guy full in the face. His nose explodes. She leans over him and spits at him. 'Mother*fucker*!' she howls, and kicks him again.

'C'mon, Janie,' says Thurston softly. 'Let's call the police.'

'No!' Janie jabs a finger in Thurston's chest. 'No fucking police! Have you got that, Cody? No police!'

'OK, Janie. Whatever you want. No problem.'

He guides her back to the door of the V. Sofi and Barb appear in the doorway, their shadows dancing across the body of the fallen giant.

'Jesus,' says Barb. 'Is he dead?'

'I fucking hope so,' says Janie, and she pushes through into the bar.

'This is bad,' says Sofi. She puts a hand on Thurston's arm. 'What does Barb want you to do?'

'I'm getting those lowlifes out.' Thurston looks at Sofi and raises his eyebrows in a question.

'What?' says Sofi.

'Are you going to tell me?'

'Tell you what?'

'What all that stuff was back inside with your beardy friend?'

Sofi's eyes flash. 'He's no friend, Thurston.' She turns back and starts walking towards the kitchen.

'So that's it?' says Thurston.

Sofi stops.

'Be careful,' she says.

CHAPTER 7

THURSTON WALKS DIRECTLY ACROSS to the group of Americans and Russians, takes the drink out of the hand of Black Goatee and jerks a thumb at the door.

'Get the fuck out. Right now. All of you.' The American starts to speak but Thurston talks across him. 'No. Nothing to say. Get out before I hurt you. If that overgrown bear you've been hanging around with is still alive, take him with you. He's in the alley considering his life choices.'

Black Goatee looks steadily at Thurston. Behind him, the Russian is thoughtful.

'Come on, Nate,' says the Russian. 'We don't need this, right?'

Black Goatee waits a couple of beats. 'OK, *cobber*,' he says, smiling. 'We'll go.' He waves a couple of his boys towards the alley. 'Go get Axel.' He turns back to Thurston.

'Listen, man. No hard feelings, OK? We're all grown-ups here, right? You ever need a job, call me. Always on the lookout for someone who can add experience to the company.' He holds out a hand. 'Nate Miller.'

Thurston looks at Miller's hand as though it's been dipped in manure. 'I wouldn't touch your hand if you were pulling me out of the wreckage of a burning plane. Get the fuck out of here before I lose my temper properly and embarrass you in front of your dickwad buddies, *Nate*.'

'OK, chief,' says Miller. 'All I'm gonna say is you might have call to regret that decision someday.' He pulls back his jacket to show the handle of an automatic tucked into his waistband.

'Good for you. SIG Sauer SPC 2022, nine nineteen,' says Thurston. 'I wondered what model it was. Must be kind of awkward walking round with one of those stuffed in your panties. Although I guess there's plenty of room down there. You ever use that thing or is it for decoration only?'

Miller nods as if Thurston has confirmed something. 'Not bad,' he says. 'Not bad at all.' He holds Thurston's gaze for a few seconds before brushing past, followed by the rest of his crew.

He is almost to the door when he spots Sofi huddled with Janie and Barb behind the bar. 'You and me got some unfinished business, ice queen. You dig?' Miller smiles and cocks his fingers into a gun. 'Bang, bang.'

CHAPTER 8

'YOU GONNA TELL ME now?'

Thurston and Sofi are the only ones left at the V. Barb's gone to bed and Janie's been put in a taxi back home. She continued to refuse any contact with the police. Thurston's locked up the darkened bar and is leaning against a steel table watching Sofi make her final clean-up in the kitchens.

'Tell you what?' Sofi doesn't look up from her task. Her arm sweeps back and forth furiously. Thurston waits patiently for her to slow down.

'C'mon, Sofi,' he says. 'You know exactly what I mean. You've got history with the guy with the beard. Miller.'

Sofi stands upright and breathes deeply. Her dark eyes glitter. She's been crying.

'OK,' she says. She puts down the cloth and runs the back of a hand across her brow. 'I know him, yes. From Reykjavik. A long time ago.' She takes off her chef's jacket and hangs it on a peg.

'And?' says Thurston.

'And what?' Sofi pulls up a stool at the table and opens her ledger. 'It is late, Thurston, and I still have to do tomorrow's orders for Barb.'

'I'll quit bugging you if you give me some more information.'

'This isn't a movie, Thurston. Miller is bad news. OK? This I can tell you. Very bad news. And you being a big hero man didn't help anything, you know? Not a thing. In fact, if I'm honest, it makes things worse. We done? I can finish my work now?'

Thurston pushes himself upright from the table. 'OK, Sofi. I'm done. I don't know why I'm asking. We won't see Miller again.'

Sofi shrugs. 'Maybe.'

Thurston stops in the doorway. 'You good to lock up on your way out? How're you getting home?'

'I have my motorbike.'

'OK. Goodnight, Sofi. And, so you know, I wasn't being any kind of hero out there. I did what I had to, nothing else.'

He opens the kitchen door.

'Thurston?' says Sofi.

He turns back and sees tears welling in the corners of her eyes. 'Yes?'

'Miller . . .'

'Miller what?'

Sofi Girsdóttir shakes her head. 'Nothing. Forget it.'

CHAPTER 9

THURSTON IS WOKEN BY a monster prowling outside his room.

He hears someone screaming, and opens his eyes to see fingers of flame creeping round the edges of his door. Below, a malevolent red line throbs. His room is full of smoke from the ceiling down to about two feet from the floor. An ominous restless roaring comes from the landing. The fire sucks up every available scrap of oxygen, gathering its strength for an all-out assault on his room at the apex of the house – the worst place possible in this situation.

Coughing out smoke, Thurston rolls out of bed, dropping onto his elbows. The floor is hot to the touch.

A woman screams and Thurston hears the door to his room start to buckle. He has seconds, no more.

Another scream. A sound from hell.

'Barb!' shouts Thurston, and he chokes on a lungful of smoke. Coughing, his eyes tearing up, he crawls to the bathroom and finds the bath taps. He drags the towels under the water and soaks them. He wraps one round his head and another round his upper body. When he turns back to his bedroom, flames are licking hungrily under the bottom of the door. The pressure from the inferno on the landing bends the flimsy wood. If he opens the door to get down to Barb, the backdraught will blow him straight through the opposite wall. And keeping the door closed won't be an option much longer.

He can't hear any more screams from Barb but knows he has to try something. He makes his way to the window and punches out the glass, his hand wrapped in a T-shirt. Smoke is sucked upwards, giving him momentary relief, but the ventilation creates a sudden rise in oxygen. The fire on the landing howls in fury and renews its assault on the door.

Thurston steps out onto his tiny balcony and looks down. Barb's room, one floor below, has an identical balcony some two yards to his left. Flames are already rolling upwards and over her window.

Thurston doesn't hesitate.

He makes the calculation and leaps down, landing square on Barb's balcony. The old concrete threatens to pull away from the brick wall but it holds. Just. The heat here is intense. Thurston puts his back to the wall, the bricks hot against his skin.

'Barb!' he shouts. '*Barb!*'

Nothing.

He braces himself. He ducks as low as he can and tries to look inside.

It's like looking into a blast furnace. Even with the wet towel wrapped around his face, Thurston's hair soon starts to smoulder.

'Barb!' he screams but gets nothing back. He knows Barb Connors is dead already and that he won't be far behind if he doesn't get off this balcony. The concrete shifts below his feet and Thurston feels the whole structure start to give. The V is disintegrating around him.

Above him, the fire outside his bedroom finally breaks down the door, and a massive backdraught blows a spume of glass and wood and flame into the cold night air. The blast knocks Thurston off balance. He stumbles dangerously, inches from tumbling over the edge of the balcony.

Sixty feet below is nothing but hard pavement.

He registers people running across the street. Someone screams and Thurston feels the skin on his fingers start to burn. In a second or two he won't be able to hold his grip. Things become simplified at these moments: do something right *now*, or die.

Adrenaline works differently in different people.

Cody Thurston has always found when his adrenaline spikes, events around him slow to a crawl. So long as that slowness is not accompanied by paralysis, it can be a useful trait. In the sliced seconds of time he has left on the balcony, Thurston scans his surroundings for an out.

There'll be something. There has to be.

And then he sees it. Not much but it's all he's got: a phone line bolted into the crumbling brickwork a yard or so down to his left. It's too far to reach with his free arm but, by swinging across and down, using his own body weight as a pendulum, Thurston manages to hook his feet around the wire. He locks his ankles together, takes a deep breath and lets go of the railing.

For a dizzying second he drops before the wire cuts into his ankles but he holds on. Now he's hanging upside down from the burning building. He swings upwards and manages to grab on to the wire. He clings to it like a monkey on a vine.

A slab of masonry topples from above and almost swipes him out of the sky.

'Move!' shouts a voice from the street and Thurston hauls himself hand over hand towards the steel telephone pole across the street. He's about twenty feet from the V when he's almost jolted off as a second piece of debris falls from the roof and bounces onto the wire. Thurston redoubles his efforts and, with each passing second, gets closer to safety.

Less than ten feet from the telephone pole, the wire finally pulls free from the crumbling brick and Thurston is free-falling. He smashes backwards into the steel pole and the wire almost jerks loose from his hand. He falls another ten feet before he's pulled up with a violent jerk as the wire finds its length.

The wire snaps and now Thurston is falling again. He twists in mid-air and lands heavily on the roof of a car parked below. The sheet metal crumples and every last ounce of Thurston's breath is knocked from his lungs.

But he's alive.

As the buzz of unconsciousness closes in, he hears a rumble. He looks across at the V in time to see the roof collapse in an explosion of dancing orange sparks and blackened timber.

And then there is darkness.

CHAPTER 10

LIGHTS. VOICES. THE CLANG of metal equipment and that unmistakeable antiseptic tang in the air. A gurney rumbles down a corridor, wheels squeaking on the rubberised flooring.

Hospital.

Thurston opens his eyes to see a young cop sitting next to the bed, his head bent over a phone, mouth slightly open.

'Is she OK?' says Thurston. 'Barb?'

The cop looks up, startled. 'What?'

'Barb Connors. She was in the pub. Did she get out?'

The cop doesn't answer.

'She didn't, did she?' Thurston lets his head sink back and closes his eyes. An image of Barb trapped inside her room comes into his mind. She's screaming, her clothes on fire. Thurston opens his eyes again and now there's a doctor leaning over him with a syringe.

'Wait,' says Thurston, but the needle is already in his arm.

'How long will he be out for?' says the cop.

The doctor shrugs. 'Six, seven hours maybe.'

'Tell m—' says Thurston but he can't complete the sentence. He feels as though he's underwater with some great beast dragging him down into the depths. He fights to keep his eyes open but it's no use. Blackness creeps in at the edges of his vision and his last coherent thought as he sinks back into unconsciousness is to wonder why there's a cop in his room.

CHAPTER 11

THURSTON'S IN HOSPITAL FOR three days. He banged himself up pretty bad getting out of the V but it mostly looks worse than it is. He's got nine stitches in a head wound and five more in his right hand. There's been some low-level skin damage on one side of his face. No broken bones. He'll live. The concussion was what concerned the doctors most. Despite the fall being broken by the car roof, Thurston hit hard. Internal bleeding was a distinct possibility but that has not shown up.

As soon as he's given the all-clear he dresses in the jeans, T-shirt and sneakers given to him by the cops and two of them sign him out and take him in handcuffs to a patrol car. No one has answered any of his questions about Barb Connors and he's been allowed no visitors. The patrol car takes him directly to Paddington Green police station, less than a mile from the hospital.

Inside the station, Thurston is shown into an interview room and left to wait. He takes a seat on one side of a plain wooden table. Now he's away from the hospital, anger about his treatment is growing. They can't think he had anything to do with the fire, so why all this heavy-handed stuff? He wonders if it could be related to something in his military past – the fire at the V bringing him to the attention of some shadowy black ops outfit. Almost as soon as he's thought of it he dismisses it as fanciful. Thurston knows too that these kind of mind games are part of any interrogation process. Whatever's happening, his conscience is clear.

Eventually the door opens and two plain-clothes cops come in. One of them, a beefy-looking guy with thin reddish hair and what Thurston guesses will be a permanently flushed face, sits down and places a file on the table in front of him.

'I'm DS Hall,' he says. 'This is DS Morrison. We'll be conducting this interview.'

Morrison is a tall, bland-looking man in his early thirties. He says nothing and takes a seat next to Hall.

'You ready to tell me what all this is about?' says Thurston. 'I need to know if Barb Connors survived.' He keeps his voice level, respectful. No sense in pissing these guys off if all they're doing is their job. Still, Thurston has to repress the urge to shout.

'Interview commences twenty-one fourteen, Monday, eleventh of January,' says Hall. He shows no sign of having heard Thurston speak. 'DS Hall and DS Morrison present. Subject, Cody Michael Thurston, formerly of 21 Hackney Road, London.'

Thurston looks at Morrison but, seeing nothing there, he keeps his mouth shut. There's a play going on here and Thurston can wait.

'Why did you do it, Thurston?' says Hall. 'She knock you back? You try and screw her and she wasn't having any of it?'

'Excuse me? What are we talking about? *Barb Connors?* She's eighty years old.'

'He's not talking about Barbara Connors,' says Morrison. 'At least, not yet.' He looks down at the file. 'We want to know why you raped and killed Sofi Girsdóttir.'

'What?' Thurston sits up straight.

Hall makes a show of sighing. He exchanges a weary look with Morrison. 'Is this how you're playing it, Thurston?'

'Playing what?'

Hall leans forward and props his elbows on the desk. 'Sofi Girs-dóttir, your co-worker and ex-girlfriend—'

'My what? Sofi's not my ex.'

'We understand you had a prior sexual relationship with her which ended recently.'

'We went out once or twice. It didn't work so we stopped. She's not what I'd call an ex.'

Hall leans further forward. 'Was the fire an afterthought? Some-thing to cover your tracks after you'd raped and killed Sofi?'

'Let me get this straight,' says Thurston. 'Sofi's dead?'

Without warning, Hall slaps Thurston across the cheek. Thurston bites back the instinct to ram Hall's face into the table. He sees Morrison tense and thinks, *He's not entirely on board here.* It's useful information.

'OK,' says Thurston. 'You can have that one, Hall.' He wipes blood from his cheek. His head wound has reopened. 'Let's do things your way.'

'While you've been in hospital pretending to be hurt,' says Hall, 'we've been busy out here building a nice, shiny, completely airtight case against you. Want to hear how it goes? After the pub shut down for the evening, you tried it on with Sofi Girsdóttir. Maybe you weren't happy about her breaking up with you. Maybe you are the kind of man who can't control himself around women. Who the fuck knows? But you tried and when you were rejected you raped and strangled her. Later, to cover your tracks, you set the pub on fire and staged your own escape. Barbara Connors, an elderly lady, your boss, was left to burn alive.'

Hall pauses for emphasis and holds up a hand. He counts off on his fingers as he talks. 'We have a petrol can with your prints on it. We have multiple witnesses who saw you arguing with her on the night of the attack. We have sexually threatening emails from you on Girsdóttir's computer. We have you alive and her dead. So, let's keep things nice and simple, shall we? Tell us why and how and it'll go easier on you, Thurston. Not much, but easier.'

Thurston says nothing.

'No request for a lawyer?' says Morrison.

'He's upset, DS Morrison. I think he might cry.'

Thurston stares at a spot on the wall somewhere past Hall's shoulder, trying to put together something coherent from the information he's receiving. Barb's dead. Well, he knew that already. He heard the screams. Sofi being dead is a shock. And the crap about him raping her is doubly shocking. Thurston thinks about the evidence Hall recounted. He thinks about that quite a bit.

It's the reason why he's not going to ask for a lawyer, because the torrent of shit coming out of Hall's mouth means one thing and one thing only: this is a grade-A stitch-up. There's no point in Thurston protesting his innocence, no percentage gained in whining.

If someone's putting this much effort into framing him then he has to come up with something better than asking for a lawyer. No, Thurston keeps quiet because he isn't planning on sticking around.

Still, there could still be advantages to talking.

Putting your opponent's mind somewhere else, for example. Thurston wants something from Hall but needs him off balance to get it.

'How much are you getting, Hall?' says Thurston. 'Enough?'

Hall frowns. 'Come again?'

'For the frame,' says Thurston. He switches his gaze to Morrison. 'You know about this too? Wait, no, I'm guessing not.' Thurston smiles bleakly and holds Morrison's gaze. 'Your partner's for sale, Morrison. A cheap whore. There must be a part of you, deep down, that knows the little fucker's dirty, right?'

Morrison glances at Hall and Thurston sees the barb has hit home. Morrison isn't in on this – whatever 'this' might be – but has enough suspicion about Hall already to figure he could be bent.

'Ah,' says Thurston, 'you do.'

'Very funny, Thurston,' says Hall. He leans forward close enough for Thurston to smell the cigarette smoke on his breath. 'You're going down, dickhead,' he whispers. 'For a long time. And you know what they do with rapists inside.'

Thurston lunges at Hall, grabbing him by his lapels and pulling him across the table. He moves so quickly, he and Hall are on the floor of the interview room before Morrison can react.

Thurston and Hall grapple for a few seconds before Morrison hauls Thurston off his partner. Hall staggers to his feet and punches Thurston hard in the stomach. Thurston drops.

'Steve!' spits Morrison. 'Enough.'

Hall, breathing heavily, controls himself with difficulty. He brushes his thinning hair back into place and adjusts his tie. Thurston is curled on the floor in a foetal position.

'Interview terminated,' says Hall.

He knocks on the door and two uniforms step in.

'Overnight,' says Hall, bending over Thurston. 'And we'll get you a lawyer, Thurston. You're not getting off on some technical bullshit.'

Thurston says nothing. Instead, he concentrates on slipping the mobile phone he's taken from Hall's pocket into his sock. He'll need it later when he gets out of here and comes after every last motherfucker responsible for the killings of Sofi Girsdóttir and Barb Connors.

CHAPTER 12

ONCE HE'S DOWN IN the cells, Thurston's chances of escape will reduce drastically. At the very least, Hall's phone will be discovered.

No, if he's going to get out of here, there's only going to be one opportunity: on the short journey between the interview room and the lower cells while the two cops taking him there assume the action is over. Slumped between the two uniforms, he waits until they pass the fire exit door. The cops aren't expecting any trouble from the hobbling Thurston so when it comes he meets little resistance. They haven't even cuffed him.

Big mistake.

Without warning, Thurston drives the point of his elbow full into the gut of the cop to his left and pops the knee of the other with a simultaneous downward heel kick. With both men disabled, he smashes the fire alarm glass and pushes open the exit door. The bare concrete stairwell is empty but won't be for long. Thurston walks slowly down, pretending to look at Hall's mobile. Cops begin to stream into the stairwell, barely giving Thurston a second glance. Lesson one in the dark arts he's been trained in: if you look as though you belong somewhere, no one questions it, not even cops.

This strategy does have a fault: it is strictly a short-term solution. The fire alarm Thurston triggered to cause confusion works well. But by the time he gets to the fire exit door at the foot of the stairs he can detect a shift in the information spreading through the cops milling around outside. News of his escape is in the air. He hears voices raised, sees fingers pointed his way.

Time to go.

Thurston moves to the kerb and waits a few seconds for what he wants on the Harrow Road. Behind him he sees five or six cops moving towards him.

C'mon, c'mon.

A courier on a big scrambler weaves slowly beside a stationary BMW. Thurston steps out into the road and, in a swift movement, drags the courier backwards off his bike.

'Stop!' yells a voice.

Thurston jumps onto the bike and guns it through the crowd of cops on the pavement. Without hesitation he roars straight down the steps of the Joe Strummer Subway, ducks under the Westway and comes up the other side heading south on the Edgware Road. By the time the first pursuit vehicle has been alerted, Thurston is at the northern edge of Hyde Park. He turns in through the gates and dumps the bike in a clump of trees. At a park cafe he swipes a blue zip-up windcheater and a baseball cap from the coat rack near the door.

Brim down, collar up, Thurston walks east towards the West End.

Six minutes after exiting Paddington Green, he's in the wind.

CHAPTER 13

OLD HABITS DIE HARD. Thank Christ.

From Hyde Park, Thurston makes his way on foot to the rear of a gym at the side of St Pancras station. He counts nine bricks up and nine along from the western corner, puts a finger in a crack in the mortar and levers out a small plastic bag. Inside is the key to a locker stationed next to the Eurostar terminal.

Even though he's been out of the game for a decade, Thurston's kept a go-bag in the locker for the past two years. The bag contains a passport in the name of Michael Flanagan, a smartphone and charger, two thousand in cash and a clean credit card, also under the name of Flanagan. The account the credit card charges back to has better than two hundred grand sitting there – the pay-off for some security work Thurston did in Mozambique after leaving the forces. He didn't do anything illegal, but the payment and the client left a bad taste in his mouth. He stowed the cash in the Flanagan account and told himself he'd only touch it on a rainy day.

Right now it's pouring down.

Thurston takes the bag from the locker and walks south from St Pancras, stopping on Tottenham Court Road to buy a laptop and a holdall. He fills the holdall with clothes bought at the first department store he finds. He also buys a navy business suit and a pair of black brogues, and tops the purchases with a heavy overcoat and scarf, dumping the clothes he's been wearing in the store dressing room. At a walk-in hair salon in Soho he gets his collar-length blonde hair dyed black and cut short. The stubble he usually wears is shaved clean. At a large chain pharmacy he buys a pair of glasses with plain lenses. By 4 p.m., the Cody Thurston who escaped from Paddington Green that morning is almost unrecognisable.

Thurston takes a train to Heathrow and books into a chain hotel in sight of the runway. Airport hotels are the perfect place to hide. Too many people coming and going for anyone to get suspicious. In his room, he charges his phone and laptop, orders some food from room service and settles back on the bed to examine DS Hall's phone. One message in particular gets Thurston's attention, as does Hall's calendar. He opens his new laptop and spends three hours researching the information on Hall's phone. Around ten he turns off the lights and tries to sleep.

The next few days are going to be busy.

CHAPTER 14

FRIDAY AFTERNOON. THE END of a nightmare week.

Two days after Thurston's escape and Steve Hall has got precisely nowhere in tracing the Australian. Hall's superior officer, DCI Venn, flays him alive and tells him in no uncertain terms to get a result, or else get ready for a long stint down in Records.

'This is a departmental embarrassment, Hall. A man under your watch – a killer, no less – waltzes out of Paddington Green in broad daylight. Have you any idea of the mountain of shit I'm having to wade through because of this? Get him found and make it quick or I'll bury your pathetic fucking career so deep you'll need an archaeologist to find traces.'

It's enough to drive a man to drink. Or, in the case of DS Steve Hall, to 22 Logandale Lane.

From the outside, 22 Logandale Lane looks like any other semi-detached in a quiet street off the Fulham Road. To those in the know, the house is one of West London's wildest knocking shops with specialities in rent boys, pain and coke, all of which tick Hall's recreational boxes. And since Hall's patch covers the area, he can come and go as he pleases, his admission costs taken care of by ensuring what goes on inside number 22 doesn't come to the attention of the police.

By eleven fifteen, Hall, wearing only a blindfold with a gag in his mouth, is tied face down on a bed. Work, DCI fucking Venn and the entire debacle of Thurston's escape is forgotten. Hall's treated himself to Raúl and Ricky, two of his favourites, and between the three of them they've made serious inroads into a baggie of top-class blow. Life, temporarily, is sweet.

CHAPTER 15

THURSTON COMES INTO THE room carrying a short-handled metal baseball bat. He puts a finger to his lips and indicates to the two naked rent boys that they should remain where they are. He takes out Hall's mobile and shoots a short video, making sure he includes both boys and Hall. When he's finished he jerks a thumb at the door. Neither boy hesitates. They recognise real trouble when they see it. Gathering their clothes from an armchair, they slip noiselessly into the corridor.

Thurston clicks the lock shut behind them, although, after the forthright conversation he's had downstairs with Mrs Murgatroyd, the owner of number 22, he doubts anyone will be riding in to rescue DS Hall any time soon. Somehow, Mrs Murgatroyd has been left with the distinct impression that Thurston works for the O'Learys – a legendary south London outfit, the mere mention of whom causes even hardened criminals to reassess their priorities.

He pulls off Hall's blindfold and the cop twists his head to one side. His eyes widen as he sees Thurston.

'Hi,' says Thurston. 'Remember me?'

He shoots some more footage of Hall's panicked face and pans across to the cocaine paraphernalia on the bedside table. Replacing the

mobile in his pocket, he picks up the baseball bat and, without pre-
amble, cracks it down hard across Hall's shoulder, breaking his collar
bone. Hall's anguished cries are mostly muffled by the gag in his mouth.
Thurston waits patiently for the man to regain some composure.

'Just a taster, Hall,' he says. 'To get you focused. I'm going to ask you
some questions and you're going to answer them.'

Hall responds angrily, spittle foaming round the sides of the gag.

Thurston hits him again on the same spot and Hall sobs.

'Wrong response. You need to concentrate. My offer isn't all warm
and fuzzy. There are no grey areas. You tell me what I want to know
and you live. You don't tell me and I'll kill you right here. You can tell
I mean this, right?'

'Yeah,' grunts Hall. 'Jesus!'

'Mrs Murgatroyd has been persuaded to give us some time,' says
Thurston. 'So, when I take the gag out of your mouth, keep quiet.'

Thurston removes the gag and Hall whimpers. 'How did you find
me?' he croaks.

'Your phone. And some research. It wasn't difficult. Now, concentrate on the matter in hand. Think of your kids, Hall. Little Timmy
and baby Natalie. And your wife, Sarah. You don't want news of this
filth getting out there, do you?'

Hall shakes his head.

'Who framed me?' says Thurston.

'They'll kill me if I tell you,' says Hall.

'I'll kill you if you don't. Your choice. Was it Miller?'

'Who?'

'Don't,' warns Thurston, and shows Hall the end of the baseball bat.

'Yeah, OK,' says Hall. 'It was Miller.'

'Tell me why.'

'The girl. She knew him back in Iceland. Knew what he does. She was a loose end.'

'What does he do?' says Thurston.

'Miller and the Russians run a syndicate. Both sides use a joint Miller's got in Iceland as a . . . as a kind of staging post.'

'For what?'

'Pseudoephedrine,' says Hall. 'Big quantities. Like, industrial. Pseudoephedrine is—'

'I know what it is. Why me?'

For the first time since Thurston came into the room, Hall shows something other than pain and panic on his face. He smiles, or tries to. 'You weren't supposed to survive. So when you did, Miller moved quick to make sure you were the perfect patsy. Foreigner. A drifter. Who gives a shit?'

'I do,' says Thurston. He stands and replaces Hall's gag. Hall tenses.

Thurston produces Hall's mobile and shows it to the cop. He types a short message containing Hall's name and rank and the location of number 22 and puts in three numbers – Hall's boss, Hall's wife and the news desk of a particularly vicious tabloid – attaches the video clips of Hall and presses 'send'.

'So long,' says Thurston and, leaving Hall thrashing impotently on the bed, steps out of the room.

Next stop, Reykjavik.

CHAPTER 16

AS MICHAEL FLANAGAN, CODY Thurston has no problem getting into Iceland, although he is mildly surprised not to see any of Nate Miller's people on the plane or at Keflavik Airport.

Leaving Hall alive was a deliberate ploy. Thurston assumed the cop would inform Miller of the encounter. From the absence of a tail, either that hasn't happened or Miller's people are better at surveillance than Thurston gave them credit for.

On the whole, he is coming to the conclusion Hall might have kept quiet, at least as far as Nate Miller is concerned. Perhaps he's overestimated Hall's ties to the American. It's disappointing: flushing out surveillance was the only thing stopping Thurston killing Hall. Now it looks as if he'll have to track Miller the hard way.

At Keflavik Airport, Thurston picks up a specialist, winter-equipped Land Cruiser he rented online last night, using the Flanagan credit card. If the drive into Reykjavik is anything to go by he's going to need it. The exposed highway heading west into the city runs along a peninsula bounded by the Atlantic on both sides. Today is darker and colder than a bailiff's heart and blowing a gale.

Or, in Icelandic terms, a stiff breeze.

Thurston battles the ice and wind into Reykjavik, stopping at a sporting goods store on the outskirts of the city to plug some holes in his gear. It's when he's coming out of the store off the Reykjanesbraut road he picks up the tail: a black Mercedes four-wheel drive parked outside a closed office block on the opposite side of the car park. A thin cough of white exhaust betrays the idling engine, the car angled so Thurston's vehicle is visible in the rear-view mirrors. It could be coincidence, but Thurston assumes that's not the case.

Thurston is impressed Miller's guys have remained undetected for so long but it's a timely reminder for him to up his game. He gets into the Land Cruiser and pulls back onto the main road, keeping the Merc in his peripheral vision.

In the city, Thurston puts the Land Cruiser into an underground car park and heads on foot to his accommodation, an apartment near the city centre. He picks up the keys from a lockbox and lets himself into the block. It's a bland one-bedroom flat with a small kitchenette and all the charm of a dentist's waiting room, but Thurston doesn't plan to stay. This apartment is window dressing.

Locking the apartment behind him Thurston exits through a side door leading to a back alley. Dropping to one knee, he levers a wooden board out from the side of a set of small steps leading from the door. He stows his backpack in the crawl space underneath and replaces the board. He walks into the alley and takes a wide circle through the quiet white streets until he comes back to the underground car park where he left the Land Cruiser. Five minutes later he's parked unobtrusively in a line of cars, watching the black Merc.

CHAPTER 17

THEY MAKE THEIR MOVE around twelve.

Three big guys, bulky in winter coats and boots, step out of the Merc. Their rising breath is caught in the light from a street lamp as they walk calmly towards the apartment block.

They're earlier than Thurston figured but he guesses, in Iceland, the hour is late enough. It won't get much quieter if they leave it until two or three and it won't get light until gone nine. That's one thing about Iceland in winter: they get plenty of night to play with.

When the men reach the apartments, Thurston loses sight of them in the shadows. He sits back and waits for them to realise he's not inside.

Sure enough, less than sixty seconds after breaking in, the three men come back into the deserted street. They don't waste any time talking – the temperature outside must be somewhere around minus twelve. Thurston, sitting in the darkened Land Crusier with the engine cold, is glad he stocked up at the sports store. Even so, it's difficult to resist turning the ignition. The men clamber back into the Merc and there's a pause as – Thurston guesses – they discuss what to do next. His hope is they'll call it a day and head back to wherever Nate Miller might be.

The Merc pulls out and takes a right. Thurston guns the car and follows.

The Merc heads north out of Reykjavik before swinging right and taking an inland highway east. With the roads almost empty, and snow falling only lightly, Thurston's pursuit is relatively easy. Once out of the city he keeps his headlight use to a minimum, and stays as far back as he dares. He is confident he has not been tagged but there's no point in taking risks. They pass few cars, which makes the tail harder.

Despite the ice and snow the road is a good one. It's been recently cleared and the Land Cruiser feels secure on the surface. Thurston eats an energy bar and sips from a bottle of water as he drives. He has the feeling this will be a long night.

The road curves around the top of a big lake and then meanders across a wide white plain. The snow stops and the sky clears to reveal a low moon strong enough to pick out deep shadows in the surrounding fields. A kilometre or so ahead, Thurston watches the lights of the Merc. They've been driving for ninety minutes when he sees the headlights pull a sharp left. From the rise and fall of the beam Thurston guesses the road they're on now is unpaved. He pulls the darkened Land Cruiser cautiously closer and checks the GPS. As he suspects, the road is little more than a farm track. In the distance he sees lights.

Thurston's not a gambler, but if he was he'd bet heavy he's found Nate Miller.

CHAPTER 18

MILLER'S PLACE IS SMALLER than Thurston envisaged: a cluster of low industrial sheds huddled around a central farmhouse about three hundred metres from the Hvítá river, about a kilometre upstream of the thundering Gullfoss Falls. When Thurston gets out of the Land Cruiser the rumble of millions of tons of water tearing through the canyons over to his right sends a low vibration through the ground under his feet. Iceland has that feeling: that the island itself is alive.

Thurston can see why Miller's chosen this place.

It's far enough from Reykjavik to be remote yet it's on a good road which, thanks to the proximity of the popular falls, is seldom closed. Miller can be at the airport inside two hours. The geography means the farmhouse can't be approached easily without being observed. Bigger picture: Iceland's geographical position and low-key policing make it an ideal staging post for bringing pseudoephedrine into Europe from the US and Russia. Lastly – and this is something right at the forefront of Thurston's mind – is the phenomenal amount of guns in the country. For all its low crime rates, Iceland has six times more weapons per head than Britain. Nate Miller is going to be armed to the teeth.

Thurston gets back into the Land Cruiser and drives slowly back towards the car park for the falls. He puts the car hard up against a maintenance shed in a thicket of shadow. In the back of the car he strips down and hurries into a nine-millimetre-thick drysuit made of neoprene rubber. Over this he dresses in the rest of the high-grade cold-weather gear he picked up in Reykjavik.

He locks the Land Cruiser and sets out for Nate Miller.

CHAPTER 19

SOFI'S VOICE COMES BACK to him as he moves across the moonlit snow-field towards the river. *Miller is bad news.*

It reminds him to stay alert.

At the river Thurston turns upstream, keeping as close to the surging water for as long as he can. Four hundred metres from the farm he spots a fold in the contours of the land which passes close to the farm and he uses it to conceal his approach. He hunches low, thankful the snow has, once more, begun to fall.

He checks his watch: 3 a.m. He's been on the move since early morning but bats the fatigue away as a distraction he can't afford.

The fold takes Thurston to within fifty metres of the nearest structure. There are no fences around the property, which he reads as a sign of Miller's confidence.

Or, perhaps, his arrogance.

There's no craft now in getting closer so Thurston simply walks quietly across the snow, banking on the late hour and remote location meaning most inside will be asleep.

He reaches the corner of the steel shed without incident and hears a noise coming from inside. The dull throb of music echoes from somewhere in the farmhouse. Thurston turns the corner of the shed and finds his way to the door. Inside are four rows of large, spotless stainless-steel silos. The air reeks of chemicals.

Thurston quickly inspects the other two sheds and finds the set-up replicated in each. He's no expert but he assumes the silos contain part of the ingredients required for the production of pseudoephedrine. An outline of Miller's operation is forming. Import high quantities of the ingredients for pseudoephedrine from Russia to the east and the US to the west. Mix in Iceland and pour into Europe via the UK. The sheer quantities mean it is a product best concealed in plain sight. From what he's seen and heard, Miller will likely have a plausible cover story for his chemicals. The police would need to dig hard to prove criminality at this point in the chain.

It doesn't matter. Thurston has no plans to bring in the police. The information he's collecting on Miller is judged solely on how it will help him annihilate the American.

Closer to the main farmhouse the music is louder. Lights dance behind the curtains. A party is in progress. Thurston is about to try to find a better-placed window when a door opens and orange light spills out across the courtyard.

Thurston slips into a patch of deep shadow and watches as the giant he last saw unconscious in the alley behind the V emerges, buttoning his jacket as he moves. The guy heads for one of the vehicles parked under a sheltering roof.

Thurston is tempted to finish this one now. He reaches for the knife strapped to his waist, but hesitates.

Miller is the primary target here. If he fails to disable the big man immediately this could all be over before it's started.

The giant drives away and Thurston turns his attention back to the farmhouse. He walks closer to the window, his boots squeaking softly on the packed snow. He finds a crack in the curtains and puts his eye to the glass.

The farmhouse, largely traditional on the outside, has been decorated inside like Vegas. On a low white sofa which curls round a copper-hooded central fireplace, a naked Nate Miller sprawls back while two girls busy themselves on his crotch. Here and there around the open-plan room are more men with more girls. Thurston estimates the girls to be about seventeen or eighteen, and that's if he's being optimistic. A glass table to one side of the sofa is scattered with cigarettes, drug paraphernalia and two automatic handguns. A girl wearing only a white bra is unconscious underneath the table. To one side is a video camera on a tripod.

An image of a younger Sofi Girsdóttir in this room springs into Thurston's mind. He feels the cold black thing in his heart compress further until it becomes a diamond of undiluted hatred. For what he did to Barb and Sofi, Miller must be removed from the planet, it's that simple. Cops, courts, judges won't do it so Thurston will.

But the guns on the table remind Thurston tonight is not the night. If this thing is going to go the way he wants, he will have to re-evaluate his strategy. It doesn't matter how clever he is, how adept, how cunning; all it takes is one of Miller's numbskulls to get lucky – to find a split second to aim and fire – and Thurston will find himself on the wrong end of a bullet.

It's of no consequence. Now Thurston has Miller's location and – in the form of the girls – renewed fervour for the job in hand. He needs weapons. He retreats from the farmhouse and starts to retrace his steps back to the Land Cruiser.

CHAPTER 20

THE HVÍTÁ RIVER GLOWS blue-white under a scudding black sky.

Thurston takes particular care on this section: a treacherously narrow strip of rock no more than a metre wide bending round a curve in the river about four metres above the torrent. This close to the water the noise is incredible. But there's another sound too: the deeper primordial bass growl of the Gullfoss Falls a hundred metres ahead roaring like some caged beast.

Gullfoss Falls lie at one of the widest points of the the Hvítá. Above it, the canyons force millions of tons of water faster and faster along the rocks until it is vomited over and down a series of huge stone steps some fifty or sixty metres wide to rejoin the river below.

As seasoned as Thurston is, the thought of falling into the Hvítá makes him light-headed. He takes each slippery step carefully, making sure he moves slowly and deliberately.

He rounds a bend and finds himself on a slightly wider part of the path that cuts into an overhanging ledge of rock.

Blocking his path is Axel, Nate Miller's giant, the man whom Thurston knocked unconscious back in Hackney. Axel is smiling. In his left hand he holds a short-handled Uzi. From his right dangles a wicked-looking axe.

'Evening,' shouts Thurston. 'How's it going?'

The big guy doesn't reply but a second voice comes from behind Thurston.

'Keep talking, pussy. See how far it gets you with the Axe.'

Thurston turns to see Nate Miller backed by three other guys. They all have guns and all look extremely comfortable about using them. Thurston curses his arrogance in underestimating Miller. Until they appeared he had no idea he was being followed.

'The *Axe*?' says Thurston. 'Jeez, how long was the brainstorming session you bunch of geniuses took to come up with that one?'

'Pretty quick,' says Miller. 'We don't like to waste time.' He shakes his head. 'Why'd you come out here unarmed? I thought you were better than that. I offered you a *job*, man. Christ Almighty. I'm disappointed.'

'My mother often says the same,' says Thurston, weighing up his chances of disarming the Axe. 'You sound exactly like her. Although she's got a better beard than you.'

'OK,' says Miller. He waves the barrel of his auto towards Thurston. 'Take this guy's fucking head off,' he tells the Axe.

Thurston slips off his backpack and lets it fall to the ground as the giant approaches. He backs away until he feels his heels hanging over the edge of the trail. Thurston looks over his shoulder at the racing water. He unzips his jacket and lets it fall and Miller laughs.

Thurston reaches his hand around his back into the waistband of his waterproof trousers. He closes his fingers around the handle of his knife. In a smooth movement he flips the knife over and hurls it at the advancing Axel. The blade glances off the guy's temple, slicing through his woolly hat and taking a chunk out of his ear. Axel bellows in pain and comes at Thurston with the axe swinging. Thurston dodges left and right and then his feet find nothing but cold thin air.

There's a moment of electric realisation and then he falls.

In the split second before he hits the water he gulps down a last lungful of oxygen before he is greedily sucked down into the Hvítá's icy depths.

CHAPTER 21

THE COLD ALMOST STOPS Thurston's heart but the thick drysuit he's wearing underneath his clothes keeps him operational.

Just.

The power of the water is astonishing. In zero visibility he feels himself being dragged downwards as though in the maw of some giant beast. He slams hard into a rock wall and then another. It's only pure luck he hasn't been smashed into pulp inside the first ten seconds.

He gets drawn into a comparably quieter zone and takes the chance to shrug off the trousers which have been acting as an anchor. He strikes for the surface and then realises.

The falls.

In almost the same moment, some accident of the current brings Thurston to the surface. He gets a brief glimpse of the night sky and registers a noise like a jet engine before he is hurled over the first great stone step and down the Gullfoss Falls.

There's nothing he can do except hold his breath and hope.

He wraps his arms around his head as he tumbles down. He hits the bottom and comes to a brief stop. A monstrous weight of cascading water is pressing him flat against the rock. He inches forward, blindly, fighting the force pulling him down. He will likely die anyway but if he stays at the bottom of this eddy he will die sooner. It takes Thurston several agonising minutes before he feels the river take him again. Once it does, he is moving faster than ever.

Quite suddenly, he tastes fresh air as the falls spit him over another ledge. He spins and sucks in more air. This time when he hits the water he manages to keep his head above the surface. He feels a fractional easing of the speed of the current and kicks as hard as he can for a spar of snow-covered rock jutting out at an angle. As he gets closer he tries to grab hold of something but his fingers won't work properly. The rocks are slick with ice and water.

'C'mon!' grunts Thurston and he kicks again, finding strength from somewhere.

The river flicks him into a tiny eddy nestling in an elbow of rock. He digs his hands into the shale and hauls himself clear of the water, lungs burning and ice already forming on his hair and face.

He permits himself a few brief seconds before he gets to his feet.

Do nothing and die.

The cold is so intense, so all-consuming, Thurston almost laughs. He feels a drowsiness begin to descend and knows this is hypothermia showing its face. He climbs up a short bank and out across an endless white plain disappearing into the darkness. He has no way of knowing how far he's come from the point where he entered the water but he's guessing it's more than two kilometres.

He flashes on the Land Cruiser parked back by the tourist office. Warmth, shelter, life. He turns back along the river and begins to run.

It's all he can do.

CHAPTER 22

THURSTON'S BEEN MOVING AS best he can for ten minutes when it dawns on him he's not going to make it back to the Land Cruiser. He's been dragged too far downstream and the cold is slowing him down too much. If he doesn't get to shelter in the next few minutes he will die out here.

He reaches a relatively high point of land and climbs, trying to ignore the stabbing pains shooting down his arms and legs as he slithers on the snow. At the top of the rise, his breath coming hard, Thurston scrapes ice from his eyes and rubs his hands while he turns 360 degrees.

He's looking at a wilderness. A blasted snowscape bounded on one side by distant black mountains. There isn't a single visible light. The pointlessness of his situation, and the inevitability of his death, hits him hard. His breath hurts his lungs. His limbs are heavy and sleep tugs at his eyelids. It would be so good to sit down, so easy to rest on the soft snow, to close his eyes and forget all about Miller and Sofi and Barb.

And then he sees it. About two hundred metres away. An electric thrill runs through his nervous system. A chance.

A roof.

It's a farm building of some sort. A cattle shed.

There's no sign of the farm it belongs to and Thurston can't risk trying to find it. It's this stinking hole or nothing.

Dead on his feet, he stumbles the last few metres to the door, lifts the wooden crossbar lock and pushes himself inside.

A wave of beautiful, stinking, animal warmth hits him and Thurston almost faints with relief. He can't see a thing but inside the stock shed the temperature feels positively tropical by comparison with outside. His arrival is greeted with relative calm and a few disgruntled moans, as though Thurston is a late arrival on an already overcrowded commuter train.

He feels his way round, bumping into the animals as he does. One stands on his foot and he pulls it away, trying not to spook the beast. He has no idea what the animals are apart from the fact they don't seem to be cows.

In a corner of the shed Thurston comes across a stack of large thick plastic bags scattered on top of a heap of straw bales. Moving as quickly as he is able, and shivering violently, he fills one of them with loose straw. There are only minutes left before he succumbs to the cold, even in here. He stuffs his wet snow boots with straw. If he's going to survive this he'll need to walk out of here. Without the boots he won't stand a chance.

He places his boots on a hay bale and bends to fumble in the straw on the floor of the shed until he finds what he's looking for: a warm heap of fresh dung. He smears it over his skin as thickly as possible, paying particular attention to his feet and hands. When he judges himself well covered he slides into the straw-stuffed plastic bag. He finds a gap between the hay bales, drops his drysuit under him, and wedges himself in the space above, stuffing handfuls of straw to plug any gaps. He pulls another bale over the top until he is encased. He curls into a foetal position and jams his hands between his thighs.

Agonisingly slowly, stinking to high heaven, he begins to thaw, hoping he hasn't been so exposed his fingers or toes become necrotic.

After a time, unconsciousness comes.

CHAPTER 23

THURSTON IS WOKEN BY a rough wet tongue energetically licking the top of his head – the only part of him not inside the straw-stuffed plastic bag.

Feeling like death, he groans and lifts his face free of his makeshift sleeping bag. As thin early-morning Icelandic light dribbles in through the cracks in the shed wall, Thurston finds himself staring directly into the disdainful hooded eyes of a white-coated llama.

'Fuck me,' he croaks. 'Llamas.'

The llama regards him curiously and then turns away.

Thurston creaks upright and promptly vomits onto the hay bales as his stomach gets rid of the river water forced down his throat the night before. After the vomiting stops he carefully checks his hands and feet. All seem to be intact, if wracked by cramps. He hopes the cramps don't indicate irreversible damage but he doesn't dwell on it: time will tell and there's no benefit in thinking about what might happen.

He unravels his drysuit and spreads it across the straw. As the llamas gather round to inspect, he puts on the drysuit. It's like climbing into a discarded bag of ice but he hopes his body heat will warm the moisture. Eventually.

Shivering, he fastens the zips and finds his snow boots. The straw has dried them a little but they are still too wet. For the second time since he got out of the river, Thurston feels the seductive tug of capitulation. Without boots he's finished. He sits down heavily on a bale and tries to force his mind to concentrate, to think.

And then, from somewhere outside, he hears a noise: an engine.

He puts an eye to a crack in the wall.

Coming slowly over the rise ahead is a snowmobile pulling a sled piled with straw bales. It turns in a wide semicircle before pulling up outside the shed.

The farmer's arrival causes excitement amongst the llamas. Their noise reaches the farmer because he calls out something in Icelandic.

Thurston positions himself behind the door and waits.

After a few seconds the shed door swings open and a heavyset man swaddled in thickly padded winter workgear walks in staggering under the weight of a bale of straw. He takes a few steps before he stops dead and slowly turns to look at Thurston over his left shoulder.

'G'day,' says Thurston and raises his hand.

The farmer looks impassively at him, as though finding a shivering, shit-covered Australian in his remote llama shed is an everyday occurrence.

'Am I glad to see you, llama farmer,' says Thurston.

As he speaks, the farmer puts down the bale, reaches into his jacket and comes out with a short-barrelled shotgun.

'I haven't got time for this,' says Thurston. He takes two quick strides forward and in one smooth motion twists the gun free of the farmer. 'If you're going to point a gun at least look like you mean it, brother, OK?'

The farmer nods.

'You speak English?' says Thurston.

'Yes. A little.'

'OK, good. I need clothes, boots, food and a car. If I don't get those things I'm going to kill you. You understand?'

The farmer understands.

CHAPTER 24

THE FARMER LIVES ALONE, which is a bonus since Thurston doesn't have to deal with the complication of a wife or family. He ties the farmer securely to a radiator and then takes a long, hot bath in the surprisingly clean bathroom. He borrows clothes and raids the farmer's kitchen, cooking a gigantic plate of eggs and washing it down with a gallon of coffee.

Less than an hour after arriving at the farm, with the farmer's confiscated shotgun nestling in a holdall on the passenger seat, he bundles the farmer into the back of his ancient truck, blindfolded and gagged. He could simply leave the farmer and take the truck but that would invite complications. Easier to take him to Reykjavik and let him make his own way back. The farmer's done nothing wrong – other than point a shotgun – but Thurston can't rule out a link with Miller, who is, after all, a neighbour.

Before heading back to the city, Thurston checks the Land Cruiser at Gullfoss Falls. As expected, it's gone. He thinks about heading straight back to Miller's place but dismisses it. With Miller assuming he is dead, Thurston knows he temporarily has the upper hand. Better to go back when he's fully prepared.

He points the truck east and heads to Reykjavik. The journey passes uneventfully although he has to blink himself awake more than once.

Eight blocks from his rented apartment, Thurston parks the truck. He grabs the holdall and steps out of the car. Leaning into the back seat, he unties the farmer's hands and walks away. By the time the old guy has his bearings, Thurston is gone.

He makes his way to the apartment and, although he doesn't expect any, checks for surveillance. Once he's satisfied Miller hasn't left anyone, he goes inside.

The place has been tossed but, since Thurston didn't spend more than five minutes there, he has nothing to worry about. He retrieves the backpack he stowed under the outside steps last night.

By midday he's in another scalding bath at the CenterHotel Arnarhvoll overlooking the harbour. He stays there for almost an hour before wolfing down a room-service steak and sleeping the sleep of the dead.

CHAPTER 25

FOR THREE DAYS THURSTON licks his wounds at the Arnarhvoll. His main concern was his hands and feet but they seem to have come through without any lasting damage. He's copped a black eye, bruised ribs and an impressive line-up of other bruises from the battering he took in the falls. As he recovers he spends time mapping out an approach route to Miller's farm and rents a car to replace the Land Cruiser. He'll report it stolen when he's left Iceland. *If* he leaves Iceland.

Thurston's dreams are plagued by images of Sofi Girsdóttir and Barb Connors – Sofi appearing to him wearing the look of pure animal horror when she saw Miller in the bar. With Barb it is her screams, screams that jolt him awake in the small hours. He spends a lot of time in those hours thinking about the two women and about the party girls he saw at Miller's place. Those girls – and it's all too easy to see a younger Sofi as one of them – were as disposable to Miller as paper coffee cups. Children – or as close as makes no difference – used as toys. Thurston flashes back to the smug expression on Miller's face at Gullfoss and fixes the image in his mind.

Thurston's escape from Paddington Green has faded from the online press. He has no doubt the case is still very much alive but at least it means his photo isn't still being splashed around the media. He notes that DS Hall is no longer mentioned as leading the investigation, although, so far, there's no tabloid exposé of the video he shot of Hall at 22 Logandale Lane.

By day three at the Arnarhvoll Thurston's ready to move on Miller again. He picks up the new rental and starts assembling what he needs. The farmer's shotgun turns out to be a piece of crap so he drops it in the bay. In a tourist bar on Tryggvagata he gets a line on somewhere to score dope which, in turn, takes him to a run-down cafe in the Efra-Breiðholt district to the east – the nearest thing Iceland has to a rough neighbourhood. A few steps and a couple of false starts later, he's out by the port talking about guns to a Russian guy who works at a car repair shop. The Russian, despite his energetic sales pitch, doesn't have much stock worth shit. But beggars can't be choosers so Thurston takes a semi-automatic Zastava pistol and an Ithaca M37 shotgun from him. He buys all the ammo the guy has along with a lead-weighted police baton.

By Wednesday night Thurston has what he needs.

He pays the hotel bill and leaves Reykjavik at midnight. By two he's at Miller's place out by Gullfoss, amped up and ready.

There's only one problem. The bird has flown.

CHAPTER 26

'WHERE?'

The guy sitting on the kitchen floor shakes his head. Blood from the crack Thurston has given him spatters across the tiles. He's a big man with a beard, in his late twenties with plenty of tattoos. Thurston has him pegged as a local recruit. From the look of the guy he might have done some boxing once but he's running to fat now. Probably got a rep in Reykjavik but, fuck, we're talking Iceland here. By Thurston's standards this tub of guts is an amateur all the way up. No wonder Miller was looking to recruit back at the V if this represented the standard local issue. Thurston guesses that's why he's been left behind to look after the joint – the gangster equivalent of a janitor.

'Fuck you!' the guy snarls and says something else in Icelandic.

Thurston jams the muzzle of the Ithaca hard into the guy's mouth. He hears some teeth break.

'Don't try that "fuck you" movie shit,' he snarls. 'It doesn't work in real life, buddy, and I'm not in a forgiving mood. Where's Miller?' He pulls the muzzle back and places it flush against the guy's right eye socket.

'English, not,' says the guy, spitting blood. Thurston pulls the Ithaca back, flicks the gun round and smashes him backwards into a table with the stock of the rifle.

Thurston has no problem doing it: he remembers seeing this guy through the window getting his tiny dick sucked by one of the teens. He poured beer over her head and laughed.

'I told you,' says Thurston. He steps forward and stands over the guy, the gun aimed straight at his face. 'You speak English just fine so don't try that bullshit with me again, understand me?'

The guy looks dazed. He rubs blood from the gash on his temple.

'So, again,' says Thurston. 'Where's Miller? I know he's gone: no cars left, rooms all empty, closets empty, girls gone, the equipment in the sheds on standby. I'm guessing there's been a big shipment out and Miller's gone back to whatever hole he calls home. This is where you come in and tell me where that is.'

The guy looks round the kitchen as if expecting Nate Miller to show up.

'Miller kill you.'

Thurston's tempted to blow the guy away simply for wasting his time. He pulls the slide on the Ithaca and lifts the stock to his shoulder.

'Wait! Wait!' Miller's guy flinches and Thurston nods, lowering the Ithaca a fraction.

'Go on.'

'He's in America, OK? OK?'

'Where?'

The guy shakes his head.

'I said, where?' Thurston pushes the gun in closer.

'Vermont. He has place there. I don't know where—'

Thurston cocks the Ithaca again.

'Not far from the border! I don't know exact! Some French name. Isle de something. All I know is it's on lake. Supposed to be a chemical fertiliser plant. That's all, I swear! I swear!'

'More,' says Thurston. 'There's more.'

'The compound?' says the guy. 'The compound is called White Nation.'

'"White Nation"? You have got to be kidding me. Miller's a Nazi?'

The guy on the floor doesn't say anything but Thurston suddenly clicks on a few images: the skinhead Russian at the V, Miller's eagle wrist tattoo, the cold stare at Lenin.

'That makes things easier,' says Thurston. He looks at the guy on the floor. He represents a problem.

As if reading Thurston's mind, the guy starts speaking. 'I say nothing!'

Thurston grimaces. He can't afford for Miller to be aware of him this time. The problem is Thurston has standards – standards that separate him from the Millers of this world.

And then the guy on the floor makes the decision for him. Reaching down, he pulls out a pistol stowed in an ankle holster. He probably thinks he's being slick but Thurston blows the guy's head off before he's released the safety.

CHAPTER 27

TO SAY NICK TERRAVERDI looks pleased to see Cody Thurston would not be accurate. As Thurston slides into the corner booth Terraverdi looks like someone who's bitten into an eclair filled with dogshit.

'Jesus, you look like crap, Thurston.'

'Gee, thanks, Nicky,' says Thurston. 'Always a pleasure.'

'You're welcome.'

They're at a joint called Connolly's on South 4th Street over by the Williamsburg Bridge. It's afternoon in New York and gloomy outside with the dull promise of snow in the air.

Terraverdi is a trim, nervy-looking man in his mid-forties wearing a tailored business suit and glasses. He's one of those guys who seldom looks at the person he's talking to. His eyes endlessly flick round the diner as his left leg pumps up and down, his restless fingers constantly picking at labels on the ketchup bottles, or flicking microscopic traces of lint off his sleeve. What he does not look like is a seasoned FBI field agent, something he has been for the past ten years.

A waitress comes over and both men order coffee. 'Be right back,' she says. The two men watch her go and wait until she's back at the counter before starting to talk.

'How's the meditation going?' says Thurston. 'You're looking mellow as ever.'

'Very fucking funny.' Terraverdi leans forward. 'I'll give you fucking mellow. You know I can get in big trouble talking to you? My bureau chief gets wind I'm meeting a wanted felon it won't matter shit how things have been before. I'll be out on my ear, Cody. Or is there another name? I assume you're not in the country on your regular passport?'

'No,' says Thurston. 'It got burnt along with everything else.'

'In the fire.'

'Yeah, what else?'

'The fire you didn't set.'

There's a pause while the coffees arrive. As soon as the waitress is out of earshot Thurston leans forward, frowning.

'What the fuck do you think, Nicky? You think I'd be here talking to you if I did this? What did you hear? I went nuts? Suddenly flipped into a killer rapist with a taste for arson?'

'Pretty much,' says Terraverdi. He takes a sip of coffee and grimaces. 'If it's any help, I don't swallow any of that bullshit.'

'I assumed as much, Nicky.'

'And your beef is not on US soil, so maybe I was kind of overstating how bad it would be for my boss to find out. We haven't had any notification about you. When you contacted me I did some background reading. It's been a while.'

'True,' says Thurston. 'Ten years.'

Both men fall silent and regard each other thoughtfully. Terraverdi taps a finger absent-mindedly against the table. After a few seconds he leans back and opens the palms of his hands in a tell-me-more gesture.

'So . . .'

'So I need to tell my high-ranking FBI buddy maybe he's going to be hearing some things about me. Probably some bad things. Like about me killing a bunch of people up in Vermont.'

'And they're all going to be lies.'

'No,' says Thurston. 'They're all going to be true.'

That makes Terraverdi sit up straight.

'Jesus, Cody. What the fuck are—'

'Listen, Nicky, I'm not here looking for your approval. I just want someone official to take a look at things if . . . if everything doesn't turn out the way I'm hoping. I don't want this to all be for nothing if I get a stray bullet. The guys I'm dealing with are flat-out bad motherfuckers, Nicky. Killers, rapists. Christ, given the age of some of the girls I saw in Iceland, they're practically child molesters. No one's going to spend a split second mourning. And you get to shut down a sizeable North American pseudoephedrine supplier.'

'Why don't you give me the details and leave it up to us?'

'Because you'd find nothing, Nicky. From what I hear this operation is running pretty tight. Besides, there's some Waco-type vibes about the set-up and I'm guessing you don't want to be the Fed at the tail end of that kind of fuck-up? No, thought not. Listen, this is personal, I admit it. But it's also the kind of thing that's best dealt with off the books, you get me? In, out, nice and—'

'I can't hear this, Cody,' says Terraverdi.

'Hear me out. You owe me.'

There's a moment's silence while both men flash back to *that* night. The night of the firefight in Fallujah. The night Cody Thurston went right back into the bleeding eye of the storm for Nick Terraverdi, a man he'd never met before, and got both of them out alive.

'Yeah,' says Terraverdi, 'yeah, I guess I do.'

'You gonna let me take care of it?'

Terraverdi nods. 'Now tell me what the fuck it is you got yourself into.'

Thurston lays it out and, as snow begins to settle on the darkening streets of New York, Nick Terraverdi listens.

CHAPTER 28

NATE MILLER HASN'T GIVEN the Australian much thought since he went into Gullfoss but he's thinking plenty about him now. Maybe it's the sound of running water, or maybe it's the dope. Or both. Whatever it is, Thurston's face keeps stubbornly swimming back into Miller's view and Miller's not sure he likes it.

He picks up his roach and takes a long drag.

He's lying back in a cedar tub set up on a deck overlooking the lake with Mercy, the hot little Hispanic bitch Donno brought over from Montpelier yesterday. Donno'd bought her off a guy running girls out of some juvie halfway house for wards of the state too old for the kids' home. Real nice piece. Young too. Not that Miller's asking.

Mercy's about on the edge of unconsciousness. She's got her eyes half closed and a sappy smile on her face. Cute, though. Miller thinks he might keep this one around a while longer than his usual. Train her up in his ways.

'What you thinking of, daddy?' Mercy drawls in a baby-doll voice. 'Anything nice?'

'Shut the fuck up, *perra*,' says Miller. 'I hate that "daddy" shit.'

'Jeez. Touch-*ee*.'

Miller looks her way and it's enough to straighten her right out. The girl drops her eyes and shuts her mouth.

'That's right,' he growls.

He takes another toke and turns back to the lake and his thoughts on Thurston.

He did some asking around about the Australian after that dickwad Brit cop Hall fucked things up. Heard Thurston had decked two cops and waltzed out of jail smooth as you like. Disappeared into nothing faster than kiss-my-ass and then shows up in fucking Iceland looking like a completely different guy.

That took training. *Skills*.

Of course, Miller saw it for himself back at the bar in London.

A guy who can put down the Axe is someone worth taking seriously. Which is one reason Miller had the place torched. Sofi was thrown in as a bonus. No sense in having one of his cast-offs wandering around London shooting off her dumb Icelandic mouth. It all went just fine, but this guy didn't accept his fate like he should have.

And showing up at the farm right before they made the big shipment? Was that a coincidence?

A thought occurs to him, a thought that, despite the temperature of the tub, sends chills down his spine. Maybe the Australian is some kind of cop. Miller turns that one over. He was 'working' in the same joint where Sofi Girsdóttir was working. Could Thurston have been tracking the Iceland connection? Jesus Christ.

Miller rubs his mouth. *That* is a fucking idea he really hopes is just dope paranoia. If Viktor thought the same . . .

Miller shakes his head. It's bullshit. It all worked out. The Russians never knew Thurston set foot in Iceland and Miller saw the fucking guy take a dive into the falls. No one could survive that shit. He relaxes. He's got this thing all boxed off neat and tidy.

He smiles as he remembers again the guy's face as he dropped into the river and flicks the roach through the clouds of steam rising from the tub.

'Come here, baby,' he says to Mercy. 'Let's kiss and make up.'

CHAPTER 29

AT FIRST GLANCE, EAST Talbot doesn't look like much of a place.

A second doesn't improve things.

It's a small ex-lumber town lying in a fold of white hills consisting of a small grid of cross streets that straggle up and out into the woods on either side. The main highway leads to I-89 fifteen miles west. Heading east, the road crawls over a ridge of densely forested hills before hitting the New Hampshire border another fifteen miles away. East Talbot's got a bar, a diner, a farm supply store with a sideline in maple syrup products and a gallery some hopeful hipster opened five years ago selling tourist shit for tourists who never buy enough. The gas station does a sideline in canoe trips on Lake Carlson, which sits under East Talbot like an oversized teardrop. There's a motel bigger than you might expect in a town this size that dates back to more optimistic times when Lake Carlson brought in large numbers of summer vacationers from New York and Boston.

Thurston's selected East Talbot because it's the last town before Miller's place at Isle de Rousse, although, now he's here, he's wondering if he'll stick out so much he might as well paint a target on his back. But Thurston guesses he's got to start somewhere. Besides, from the look of things, East Talbot has been hit by a neutron bomb that's left the buildings but removed all trace of humanity. Since he reached the edge of town he hasn't seen a single sign of life on the slush-lined streets. A thick blanket of grey cloud sits across the town like a pan lid.

At the Top o' the Lake Motel, Thurston's rented Jeep carves black tracks across the entirely empty snow-covered lot. He pulls up next to the lobby and steps out of the car as a few flakes of snow begin to drift down out of the flat sky.

Inside two women are talking animatedly behind the counter. At Thurston's entrance, both look up, startled, as if a bear has walked in. Thurston guesses they aren't exactly overwhelmed by customers.

After a moment's pause, the older of the two women smiles. 'How you going today?' she says. Of middle age, she's wearing so much polyester Thurston's certain she'd spark a fire if she crossed her legs too quickly. 'The storm's about due so you timed this right, hey.'

The other woman is around thirty, wearing jeans and a sweatshirt with the motel logo printed above her left breast. She's got her blonde hair pulled up under a striped bandanna and is carrying a clipboard. She looks coolly at Thurston but doesn't speak.

'Well, it's snowing,' says Thurston.

He knocks his Australian accent back and tries to give the words a New York twist. It won't pass as American but he's hoping up here in Vermont they might not listen too closely. From what he's heard so far, rural Vermonters don't sound much like Americans anyway.

'I'll see you tomorrow, Lou,' says the younger woman. 'Don't forget to add detergent to Pablo's list, OK? We're all out.' She slides the clipboard behind the counter and shrugs into a thick down jacket that was hanging on the back of the office door. She acknowledges Thurston with a brief flick of her eyes and leaves.

'Bye,' says Thurston to the closing lobby door.

'Don't mind Terri. She's kind of, uh . . . well, she's Terri. Now, where was we?'

'Storm?' says Thurston, handing over a credit card.

'That's right! Big one comin', they say.' The woman swipes Thurston's card and slides it back across the counter. 'Could be a doozy! But you'll be cosy with us, Mr Flanagan. I put you in 205, second floor along to the right, Mr Flanagan. Kind of an upgrade.'

'Kind of?' says Thurston.

The woman shrugs. 'Between you and me, all the rooms are pretty much the same but 205 is on a corner. So it's a little bit bigger. And with us bein' so quiet you haven't got no neighbours. Y'can make as much noise as you like.'

'Oh, OK. Thanks.'

'You want me to pick out the sights, hon?' says the woman as she hands Thurston the keys to his room. 'Or you here on business?'

'Real estate.'

Lou's eyes light up. 'Buyin' or sellin'? Because this place is on the market, y'know. Get the right owner it could be a gold mine.'

'More of a farming type thing,' says Thurston. He shoulders his backpack and turns for the door, keen to end any enquiry into his non-existent real estate story. 'But thanks anyway.'

'OK, enjoy your stay. Oh, and we don't have a restaurant on the premises but there's a discount on meals over at the diner, and on drinks at Frenchie's.'

'Frenchie's?'

'The bar on Main? Stay there long enough and you'll meet most folks in East Talbot. I'll be there myself after eight.'

Thurston nods and pushes through the door before she goes any further.

He feels Lou's eyes on his back all the way to his room.

CHAPTER 30

LOU WAS RIGHT ABOUT the storm.

Less than an hour after Thurston checks in he watches from his corner window as the edges of the town blur. After a while all he can see through the thickening blizzard is the neon glow from Frenchie's down the street. Thurston puts on his boots, grabs his down jacket and a beanie and steps out into the motel corridor. Before he leaves he wedges a sliver of matchstick under one of the door hinges – an old trick, almost a reflex.

Outside, the temperature has dropped ten degrees. Thurston trudges across the parking lot and gets a burger at the otherwise deserted diner. When he leaves, the owner – a deadpan old boy with a lined face that puts Thurston in mind of a bulldog sucking a lemon – begins switching off the lights before the door closes.

Thurston takes a right. As he turns the corner into Main Street he cops a faceful of snow and flashes back to that night three weeks ago on his way to the V down the Hackney Road. Heading towards Frenchie's, the memory is a reminder to him to watch his step and to remember why he's here.

He opens the door to a warm blast of air and the sound of country music and conversation. A long bar is lined with customers, many of them watching the bank of six TVs, all showing sports.

'Close the goddamn door, man,' someone yells.

Lou wasn't kidding about everyone in East Talbot turning up at Frenchie's.

From what Thurston can see there are more people inside the bar than he'd have believed live in the town.

Thurston's arrival doesn't cause so much as a ripple. He was worried the place might stop dead at the sight of a stranger, and feels a little foolish when absolutely nothing happens.

There's no space at the packed bar but Thurston finds a spot at a single table in a corner. He orders a beer from the waitress and sits back, glad to be in the warmth of a bar in full flow without any of the responsibilities of working. He takes a pull on his drink and thinks again about Sofi and Barb. It occurs to him that Janie and Lenin and some of the regulars might have heard he was responsible for the fire and the deaths, and hot anger at Miller flares up once more. He hopes Janie and Lenin won't believe what they hear but he's not certain. They—

'You mind?'

Thurston looks up to see a good-looking blonde woman standing in front of him. She's indicating the empty chair across from him. It takes a few seconds for him to place her before realising she's the woman he saw talking to Lou at the motel. With her hair down and a touch of lipstick she looks different. What was her name? Jerry? Toni?

'This ain't a come-on or nothing,' she says, 'but I'm not about to spend the night standing up. I been doing that all day. No offence.'

'Sure. Be my guest,' says Thurston. 'I was, uh, miles away.'

He waves a hand at the chair. The woman takes off her outdoor coat and sinks back.

He calls over the waitress.

'Can I get you something to drink?' he says. 'This ain't a come-on or nothing.'

The woman smiles. 'I'll have what he's drinking, Darla,' she says to the waitress. Thurston sees a brief flash of something – approval? – pass between the two.

'Same again for me,' he says.

'Terri,' says the woman as Darla weaves back towards the bar. She holds out a hand and, when they shake, her grip is firm, her touch still cold from outside.

'Mike,' says Thurston. 'We met, kind of, at the motel earlier?'

'Are you asking me? Or is that the way you speak? What is your accent?'

'It's a long story,' says Thurston as Darla arrives back at the table with the beers.

When she's gone, Terri leans forwards and props her hand on her chin. 'I like long stories,' she says.

CHAPTER 31

A GOOD NIGHT. THURSTON has forgotten how they feel.

He and Terri talk and drink some beer and then talk and drink some more. He almost asks her to dance at one point before remembering in the nick of time he is Australian.

A cop comes in and Thurston sees him exchange a look with Terri. He taps a finger to his snow-dusted hat and walks towards the bar.

'Who's that?' says Thurston.

Terri rolls her eyes. 'Sheriff Riggs.' She takes a sip of beer and runs her fingers through her hair.

'He seems to like you,' says Thurston.

'Yeah, well. That's as maybe. The feeling ain't mutual. The guy gives me the creeps if you want to know the honest truth of it.' She sits back and regards Thurston. 'Y'know, if I was a gambling woman – which is a great name for a country song, right? – I'd bet you was some sort of cop.'

Thurston shrugs.

'Real estate?' says Terri. 'I can't see that. But you've got some cop thing.'

'I was in the military,' he says. He's aware he's stepping out further than he wants to, like a man inching onto a frozen lake. 'Maybe that's it.'

'Maybe. You in the military for long?'

'Let's change the subject. Is that OK?' Thurston smiles to let Terri know there's no offence taken. 'I did a few years.'

'And you don't like talking about it?'

'Something like that.'

The conversation seems to signal a shift in the atmosphere between them.

'Listen,' says Terri. 'I better go. I got a shift in the morning and I don't want to get there in bad shape.'

She stands and puts on her coat. Thurston scratches his head.

'Something I said?' he asks. He notices Riggs look up from his conversation with the bar owner and smirk. Thurston gets the idea that Riggs is not unhappy Terri's given him the brush-off.

Terri smiles. 'Goodnight, Mike.'

When she has gone, Thurston can't help but feel disappointed. Not that he was *expecting* anything exactly, but things looked to be going well. He likes Terri and he thought she liked him.

You're losing your touch, buddy, says a voice in his head. *Like you ever had it*, comes the response.

Thurston waits ten minutes before leaving himself. He doesn't want to look as if he's chasing Terri.

He walks back to the motel through four inches of snow piled on the sidewalk. The cold sobers him up although, truth be told, he hasn't had much. And he got some useful information about Isle de Rousse at Frenchie's. About how there is one road in and one road out. About the way 'the folks' up there don't come into town much and when they do they don't leave a real good impression. Nothing concrete, but Thurston is building a picture of what he's up against.

The Top o' the Lake Motel is mostly dark when he gets back. He lets himself in the lobby door and heads past the empty desk towards 205.

He is at the door, key in hand, when he freezes. He looks down and bends to pick up an object off the thin corridor carpet.

The sliver of match he placed in the door jamb earlier.

Thurston pulls the hunting knife from his belt and places an ear softly against the thin veneer of his room door.

Nothing.

He glances up and down the deserted corridor. The place is like a morgue.

He pads the few steps to room 206 and puts his ear to the door.

Again, he hears nothing. He bends to the lock and, using the knife as a lever, pops it with a soft *snick*. He waits a few seconds but hears nothing from inside.

As Lou told him, the room is empty. Thurston moves silently to the window and slides it open. A cold wind slices through the opening and he steps out onto the small balcony, trying to force back memories of stepping out onto the balcony at the V. This one is separated from the balcony outside 205 by nothing more than a chest-high piece of blockwork.

He puts one foot on the icy rail and hauls himself up and over the wall and drops onto the neighbouring balcony. He presses his back up against the stucco and peeps into 205 through a narrow gap in the curtains.

He's sees nothing except darkness.

Feeling a little foolish, and more than a little cold, Thurston's mind replays the number of ways the match fragment may have dropped clear of the door. He slides the blade of his knife into the gap between window and frame and lifts the latch. Growing more confident by the second, he slips into 205.

He's taken one step inside when he senses movement to his left and turns as someone smashes a table lamp across the back of his neck.

CHAPTER 32

MILLER'S PHONE RINGS TWICE and then goes dead.

He puts down the beer he's working on, looks up from the Canadian ice hockey game on TV and sighs. Even though two rings is what he agreed to with the guy on the other end of the line, it still bugs him when he has to do this James Bond secret code shit.

Miller digits a number and waits for the connection.

'It's me,' he says and then listens awhile. 'Tell me what Frenchie said about this guy's accent again,' he says. 'In detail.'

When he hangs up he stands for a minute looking at the figures on the ice and then dials another number.

Viktor needs to know about this.

CHAPTER 33

THURSTON GETS HIS FOREARM up quick enough to take some of the sting out of the attack. Even so, the heavy base of the lamp drops him to his knees. Before the next blow lands he manages to twist and scissor-kicks the legs from under his attacker. He hears a body land on the carpet. He flips over to straddle his opponent and brings his knife up—

The table lamp blinks on and Thurston finds himself looking down at a naked Terri Greening, her mouth set in an animal snarl.

'What the fuck?' he says.

Terri twists out from under him and grabs a sheet from the bed.

'You always come in through the fucking window?' she snarls. 'And what's with the knife?'

'You break into everyone's hotel room?' says Thurston. 'And you're lucky I didn't have a gun.' He rubs the back of his neck. 'You pack a wallop.'

'Good,' says Terri. 'I hope it fucking hurts.' She groans and rubs her leg. 'I think you broke my leg.'

Thurston gets to his feet and holds up his palms in a conciliatory way. 'Let's start over, OK?'

'Maybe.'

'How did you get in?' he says, and then holds up a hand again. 'Wait. You work at the motel. You have keys. Dumb question, right?'

'About as dumb as it gets.'

'OK. Next one. Why are you here?'

Terri Greening raises her eyebrows. 'That's possibly even dumber. Maybe I did hit you too hard.'

She steps off the bed and lets the sheet drop.

'Ah,' says Thurston.

'Right,' says Terri. 'Ah.'

CHAPTER 34

VIKTOR DELAMENKO DRIVES CAREFULLY out of Southie – no sense in getting pulled over when the trunk of the Range Rover's rattling with enough hardware to invade Canada. It's an easy four-hour pull up to Isle de Rousse, even in the snow. Miller told them to take it easy, no panic. So long as the job is done in the next twenty-four hours everything will be hunky-dory.

And Viktor's inclined to drag the thing out a little – make Miller sweat.

The simple fact of Miller bringing in Viktor and his boys in the first place is a little victory in itself. Viktor wouldn't necessarily say it to Nate Miller's face, but subcontracting this wet work, even to a sub who's a business partner, isn't a good look when his own boys are right there. Miller can justify it all he wants about not shitting in your own back yard, but it's all Delamenko can do to keep the smile off his face.

'They say why?' asks the man in the passenger seat, Dmitri Puli, Viktor's second-in-command.

Puli is ex-*Spetsgruppa A* – Alpha Group – a Kremlin true believer who, after one too many blood-and-shit details in Chechnya, stopped believing and swapped sides. Seeing his old colleagues back in Moscow cleaning up while he had his ass on the line in the North Caucasus tipped him into this line of work. Puli's a thin man who looks like a civil servant.

In the back seat, looking at his phone, is the youngest of the three, Boris Spetzen, a classic Moscow 'bull' cleaned up and put into a suit. Delamenko still checks Spetzen isn't wearing running shoes every time they go out on a job. Spetzen's there if they need any heavy lifting done but has about as much class as you'd expect from someone who's fended for himself from the age of eight.

Delamenko shrugs. 'Miller doesn't want anything traced back to his place. Says this guy might be connected.'

'To who?'

'He didn't say. Does it matter?'

Now it's Puli's turn to shrug. 'No, I guess not.'

Delamenko takes the ramp onto 93 and settles back.

CHAPTER 35

IT'S BEEN A WHILE.

Two months to be exact. With Sofi, one night after they both had a few too many shots. It was Lenin's birthday and a lock-in at the V after hours.

Thurston sinks back into the bed and crooks an arm behind his head. He lets out a long, slow breath. Next to him, Terri does the same and runs a hand through her hair.

She gets up and walks towards the bathroom. Thurston watches her. They left the broken lamp lying on the floor and it makes her shadow dance across the ceiling. At the door, aware of his gaze, she flicks out a hip like a showgirl exiting the stage.

Two months.

Sofi Girsdóttir. Thurston lets the name run through his mind and doesn't like where it takes him.

Terri comes back into the room and slides back into bed.

'You gonna tell me?' she says.

'Tell you what?'

'What you're really doing here.' She props herself up on an elbow and looks Thurston straight in the eye. 'Don't get me wrong, I don't blame you for spinning me a line. All the stuff back at Frenchie's about working in a bar and travelling around—'

'All true,' says Thurston, cutting across her.

'Yeah, O K, maybe I can buy that. But you being here, in East *Talbot* for Chrissakes. Nobody comes to East Talbot.'

'I did.'

'Hmm. Kind of my point.' She rolls onto her back. 'Jeez, I wish I smoked at times like this.'

There's a silence.

'It's the place out on the lake, isn't it?' she says. 'Up at Isle de Rousse. Talbot Chemical. That's why you're here.'

Thurston doesn't reply and rolls over on his side.

He's not doing the strong silent routine but he doesn't trust himself not to spill it all to Terri. It's been a long time since he talked properly to a woman – to anyone – and the temptation is strong. She's one of the good ones, Thurston knows simply by being here next to her. If he told her everything she'd understand. It would be fine. He could leave this thing with Miller, see how it plays out with Terri. Start again.

Instead he says nothing and the silence grows.

After a couple of minutes Terri gets dressed and leaves without another word. As the door closes behind her Thurston rolls onto his back and looks up at the ceiling.

'Shit.'

CHAPTER 36

WHEN THURSTON WAKES, EAST Talbot sits under a blanket of freezing fog. He showers and dresses quickly before heading downstairs. Lou's back on reception and gives him the frost. He wonders if she's pissed because he slept with Terri, or because Terri's spilled about what a sneaky lying bastard he is.

Outside it's colder than a hockey puck's belly. He hurries across the ghostly parking lot and into the diner for breakfast. He's working on a second pot of coffee when Sheriff Riggs comes in.

There are about half a dozen customers in the joint but Riggs makes a beeline for Thurston's booth.

Shit.

He knows he should play nice but there's something about Riggs that rubs him up the wrong way. He feels like Riggs could be from the same cop tree as Hall back in London.

'You mind?' says Riggs. He looms over Thurston and jerks a thumb at the bench opposite.

Thurston looks up. 'Does it matter?'

Riggs smiles without warmth. 'Not really. Cold as all hell outside. I need coffee.'

He slides his sizeable ass onto the vinyl and scoots along the bench until he's facing Thurston. Riggs looks across to the counter and raises a finger. Vinegar Face behind the counter must speak Riggs's sign language because he gets busy right away.

'Riggs,' says the cop. He doesn't offer a hand, which is fine with Thurston because he flat out doesn't like Riggs. He's seen these guys before.

'Flanagan,' says Thurston.

Riggs smiles. 'OK,' he says. '*Flanagan*.'

Vinegar Face arrives with coffee and a Danish pastry. He gives Riggs a microscopic glance and treats Thurston as though he's got leprosy.

Thurston drinks his coffee and waits. Riggs doesn't say anything and Thurston sits there. He knows this bullshit drill backwards. Riggs has that look on his face cops have – the kind of look that suggests they know everything about you and don't like it. It wouldn't matter a crap whether or not Thurston is polite. Riggs wants this conversation to be a warning – Thurston can see it in his eyes. The thing is, Thurston's not the type to respond. He runs a piece of toast around the egg on his plate and eats. He can do silence.

Riggs raises his eyebrows. 'You've talked to cops before, right?'

'I've met 'em.'

'You got the look.'

Thurston drains his coffee cup and reaches into his pocket. He pulls out a ten and puts it on the table. One thing about being way out in the middle of nowhere: it's cheap.

He slides across the bench seat. As he makes to get up Riggs leans forward and puts a hand on Thurston's arm. Thurston looks down at Riggs's pudgy hands.

'No offence, sweetheart,' he says, 'but I don't swing that way.'

'You were talking to Terri last night,' says Riggs.

Thurston shrugs his arm free of Riggs's grip. He stands and puts on his jacket.

'I said—' begins Riggs.

'I heard,' says Thurston. 'I just didn't reply.'

'You need t—'

Thurston walks away from the table as Riggs is talking. He exits the diner and walks down the steps onto the lot. Behind him Riggs clatters through the doors and slips on the snow. Thurston watches the cop pirouette, his arms windmilling through the air before he lands heavily flat on his ass. Riggs scrabbles to his feet with some difficulty, shoots a look of pure loathing at Thurston and slithers towards his patrol car.

As Thurston walks away he glances up and sees Vinegar Face laughing so much he's wiping tears from his eyes.

CHAPTER 37

THURSTON DRIVES TO MONTPELIER through the fog along a more or less deserted interstate. Every now and again the back of a big truck looms up out of the murk, the tail lights blurring as Thurston passes. Outside Barre he sees the flash of emergency vehicles and a towtruck winching a car onto a flatbed. Before he gets to Montpelier he sees two more crashes. It's a day to stay put but there aren't any big enough stores of the kind Thurston wants nearer East Talbot.

After an hour and a half he reaches his destination unscathed. At a hardware store he buys a cordless Grex nail gun operating off nothing more than a couple of AAA batteries. He throws in a box of two-inch nails and an Estwing double-headed axe with a rubberised grip. He could have picked up guns in New York, or maybe even nearer to East Talbot, but Thurston's decided he doesn't want to risk stumbling into some kind of ongoing anti-gun initiative. Based on what he saw at Gullfoss, he reckons on picking up more conventional weapons when he picks off the perimeter guys at Miller's compound.

At an electronics store he buys a Nikon with a decent zoom lens and a weatherproof casing. He stocks up on winter gear and various outdoor essentials at a sporting goods place next door. He shells out almost a grand for an ultra-lite TenPoint Shadow crossbow and five boxes of aluminium bolts. A pair of Sightmark Ghost Hunter night vision binoculars and a lightweight pair of Zeiss regular binoculars add to the bill. The Mozambique money is coming in damn useful.

Heading back from Montpelier, Thurston takes the long way round and winds towards Isle de Rousse from the east. This side of the ridge the road hasn't been cleared as well as it has on the western side, so Thurston's glad of the Jeep's winter rig. Coming this way means he won't be seen heading out of East Talbot in the direction of Isle de Rousse.

Two miles from Miller's compound, he pulls the Jeep onto a fire trail and bumps along through deep snow for fifty yards before parking under a low branch. He puts on his winter gear and stows the Nikon and crossbow in the backpack. Today is strictly recon but Thurston's not going to take any chances.

CHAPTER 38

THE RUSSIANS GET TO East Talbot around three and head up to Isle de Rousse as darkness creeps in. The fog hasn't lifted all day.

Delamenko turns off the highway down an unmarked road that cuts back down towards the eastern edge of Lake Carlson. About half a mile in, he slows as he approaches a gatehouse with a red-and-white-striped rising barrier across the road. As the Range Rover's tyres crunch across the snow, two men wearing jeans, sheepskin jackets and Stetsons step out of the gatehouse, both carrying semi-automatic rifles. Puli, who hasn't been here before, reaches into his jacket.

'Easy, brother,' says Delamenko, putting out a hand. 'Relax.'

'They might as well advertise "we supply drugs",' replies Puli. 'Jesus, what's the point of a cover story if they don't make an effort? At least *look* like a fucking chemical feed place. Put a sign up, wear a security guard uniform.'

'I know,' says Delamenko. 'I've talked with Miller about this before. He says he has the territory taken care of.' The big Russian shrugs. 'Americans. You know what they're like.'

'Hey,' says Spetzen, leaning forward and pointing at the approaching men. 'Cowboys!'

Delamenko stops the car and lowers the window. One of the men peers inside. Spetzen holds up his hands in mock terror. 'Don't shoot,' he says with a heavy Russian accent and smiles.

'Wait here,' says the cowboy without giving any indication he's heard Spetzen. The second cowboy walks back to the gatehouse and Delamenko watches him make a phone call.

'Miller said this would be taken care of,' says Delamenko. 'None of this gate bullshit.'

'Yeah, well,' says the cowboy, 'shit happens, I guess. This ain't Moscow, Putin.'

Puli mutters something and Delamenko raises a finger to quieten him. There's a pause during which the only sound comes from the idling car engine. Then the barrier rises and the cowboy waves them inside with the muzzle of his rifle.

'*Yesh'te der'mo derevenschina,*' says a smiling Delamenko to the cowboy as he drives through the gate.

Eat shit, redneck.

CHAPTER 39

THIS PLACE IS IN a different league to Miller's joint at Gullfoss.

That's the first thing Thurston registers. By the time he's made his first pass around the perimeter, he's reached the conclusion that this place has been built with two simple aims: to produce lots of drugs and to be easy to defend.

A twelve-foot-tall, heavy-duty electrified fence topped with razor wire sits in a U shape around the compound, with twenty yards of clear ground between it and the forest. Thurston, keeping to the trees, spots CCTV cameras every hundred yards. In the gap at the top of the U is the lake. Thurston can't get an angle on that yet but he imagines they have double or triple spotters in place there, especially in winter when the lake freezes. Inside the perimeter fence he observes two dog patrols. There's only one road in and one road out. In addition to the two guards at the gatehouse there are two more positioned to the north and two to the south where the fence meets Lake Carlson.

If Talbot Chemical Feed is a genuine company it is taking its security way too seriously.

Thurston waits for darkness.

CHAPTER 40

DELAMENKO, PULI AND SPETZEN drive past the three massive chemical storage sheds glowing pale orange under the halogens, the fog forming softly glowing globes around the floodlights. They pass the long low bunkhouse which, Delamenko knows, houses the main staff on site. He has no idea how many men are there at any time but he guesses around fifty. Maybe more. At this time of year he figures Miller will have less crew on the ground. Even white supremacists don't like the cold.

'Christ Almighty,' mutters Puli. His mood has been darkening since arriving in East Talbot. 'I don't understand,' he says, turning to Delamenko, 'why we couldn't come in, do the job and get the fuck back to Boston. Back to civilisation.'

'Miller has some special instructions. Another job. Extra.'

'*Miller, Miller, Miller,*' says Puli.

'He's the boss,' says Delamenko.

Puli says nothing.

'Don't let the cowboy shit fool you, Dmitri. Miller didn't get there being a Boy Scout. He is dangerous. And that's me telling you, understand?'

'OK, Viktor. I get it,' says Puli.

'Let's get on with it,' says Delamenko. 'Get back to Southie. I hate the country.'

CHAPTER 41

THURSTON ALMOST STUMBLES ACROSS the dead deer as he's looking for a suitable entry point. The carcass is hardly visible, covered by a crust of snow. A youngish female, her broken hind leg caught in a cleft between two logs.

He skirts around and then stops. He retraces his steps to the dead animal.

Grunting with the effort, he hauls the deer free and, as best he can, drapes the body across his shoulders. He looks across at the fence and sees he is, as far as he can tell, outside the scope of the CCTV cameras. It's dark now anyway.

Thurston walks across the open ground towards the fence. About a yard from it he lifts the creature clear of his shoulders like a weight-lifter and throws it onto the fence, leaping backwards as he does.

He's rewarded by a spectacular flash and the smell of burning flesh. As he suspected, the fence packs a punch. This is not something designed to give a mild shock.

He darts back into the trees and waits.

He doesn't have to wait too long. Less than twenty minutes has passed before he hears the buzz of a quad bike and sees the beam from its headlight bouncing across the snow on his side of the perimeter. As the bike draws closer, Thurston sees a single rider. He slides a bolt into the crossbow and takes off the safety.

The rider, a hunting rifle slung across his back, halts next to the dead deer, steps off his bike and turns off the engine.

'Shit,' Thurston hears him say.

He bends and pulls the animal clear of the fence. As Thurston hoped, the fence has been shorted by the contact because the quad bike rider has no hesitation in touching the animal. The rider drags the deer back a few more yards. He wipes his hands on the snow and lifts a torch from the quad bike. The guy sweeps the area without any sense of urgency. If he's noticed anything weird about the deer it isn't showing. Thurston guesses he's going through the motions. After a few seconds he climbs back on the quad bike and heads back the way he came.

Thurston shoulders the crossbow, breaks from the trees and reaches the fence in less than ten seconds. He pulls a small pair of wire cutters from his pocket and grabs hold of the fence.

CHAPTER 42

A QUIETER NIGHT AT Frenchie's.

Terri's at the bar with a beer, half watching a hockey game on the TV in front of her. Ellie, a friend, sits to her left and has been talking non-stop for about the last hour – which is why Terri's watching the game. The fact that Terri hasn't said much more than 'Is that right?' or 'Uh-huh' or 'I know' in that time hasn't stopped Ellie's flow. Terri's regretting calling Ellie up but Terri's not a woman who likes to drink alone. Especially when she aims to get loaded. She signals to Flynn behind the bar for another.

Terri's thinking about the Australian – if that's what he is. *Michael.* Somehow she knows that's not his real name. He was nice. Terri flashes on a couple of images from last night and a smile creeps onto her lips – a smile that gets wiped when she catches sight of the off-duty Riggs on the other side of the bar.

'What?' says Ellie, for once paying attention to Terri. 'What was so funny?'

'Nothing,' says Terri. 'I was thinking about something.'

Ellie doesn't ask a follow-up question and while she's prattling away about some new guy up in Barre, Terri thinks about the look on

Michael's face when the light came on after she hit him with the lamp and a chill runs down her spine. While her adrenaline was spiking off the charts, he looked about as calm as a man taking an evening stroll.

She doesn't know much, but she's willing to bet Michael Flanagan is not here shopping for real estate.

CHAPTER 43

NO FLASH. NO BANG. No electricity.

Thurston breathes a sigh of relief and cuts through half a dozen strands. He pulls the fence apart and steps through, making sure there's plenty of room to step back once the power's been restored. The last thing he wants is to be stuck inside the perimeter once the recon mission's done.

He crosses towards the line of trees and is swallowed up in the shadows. A couple of small animals skitter out of the way as he descends the hill towards the floodlights glowing through the fog.

An hour later and Thurston's got a pretty clear idea of where everything sits inside the compound. He's had a couple of ticklish moments when the dog patrol has passed by but rode his luck. He shoots a bunch of images on the Nikon and decides he's done enough for one night.

By midnight he's back in the Jeep and heading around Lake Carlson on his way back to East Talbot.

CHAPTER 44

'THERE,' SAYS SPETZEN. HE points across the intersection as the door to Frenchie's opens and two women walk out, one of them laughing and holding on tight to the other. Both of them look a little unsteady on their feet.

'Which one?' says Puli.

Delamenko catches a flash of blonde hair under the taller woman's woolly hat. 'The taller one. Miller said she had really blonde hair.'

'We gonna do both?' says Spetzen.

Delamenko shakes his head. 'Not unless we have to.'

He motions to Spetzen, who climbs out of the back and heads after the two women. Delamenko puts the Range Rover into gear and pulls out of the side street. He passes the two women and carries on about quarter of a mile. Spetzen's going to update them by phone.

'This is bullshit,' says Puli. 'This bitch isn't our concern, Viktor.'

'We been through this.' Delamenko doesn't move his eyes from the rear-view mirror. He wishes Puli would stop whining. It's done. Get the fuck on with it.

As if reading his mind, Puli falls silent. The two men wait.

About two minutes later, Delamenko's phone vibrates. He reads the screen and turns to Puli. 'It's on. Blondie's on her own.'

He pulls the Range Rover round in a circle and heads down Main. Puli spots the woman turning into a side street with Spetzen closing in. Delamenko accelerates towards the kerb as Spetzen grabs the woman from behind, his big hand over her mouth. Puli steps out and Spetzen shoves the woman into the back seat. He gets in, deflecting a kick and knocking her out cold with one punch. Puli gets back into the passenger seat and Delamenko pulls away.

No one sees a thing.

CHAPTER 45

SOFI GIRSDÓTTIR COMES TO him again in his sleep. This time she looks distracted. She tries to say something to Thurston but he's not listening. Frustrated, Sofi begins pulling at his sleeve. In the background he hears Barb Connors screaming but now it's at a distance.

'Come on, Cody,' says Sofi. 'Come on!'

From far in the distance comes a click and Thurston knows what it is. He's heard the sound before, many times, and it's never a good moment.

The muffled slide being ratcheted back on an automatic weapon.

He opens his eyes.

CHAPTER 46

DELAMENKO LEADS THE WAY, Puli behind him with Spetzen carrying Terri Greening over his shoulder, bringing up the rear. Using the unconscious woman's keys for the motel, the three Russians go in via the fire doors at the back and head up the stairs towards 205.

Puli's got a 9mm SIG Sauer automatic fitted with a fat piston silencer. Delamenko has a Remington semi-automatic shotgun, its muzzle also blunted by a squat silencer.

The three men move in complete silence, Puli's bitching subsumed in the requirements of what's happening. All three men have service histories; Puli's is the longest and bloodiest. They know how to do this.

In the corridor leading to 205, Delamenko pauses. From what he's been told by Miller, the guy they're here to kill has some military skills. Delamenko's pretty sure Miller hasn't been completely honest about how good those skills are. Delamenko saw for himself the guy do a pretty good job on the Axe back in London so he's taking no chances. And although it'd kill him to admit it, Puli was right about the girl being bullshit. Miller's 'added extra' – killing her and the Australian and letting Riggs tie up a neat bundle – might be one of those things that sounds like a brilliant idea but is less easy to do in practice. It's a detail they could do without. If Miller wanted them to come in and do a pro job on this Thurston guy that's fine. If he wants rid of the chick who shopped Thurston to him then why not shoot her and put her in the fucking woods? Christ, there's an industrial furnace out at White Nation. Why not put both of them in there?

Delamenko shakes his head impatiently. No sense in asking questions now. Get into the room, kill the Australian, kill the woman and get back to Southie before daybreak.

At the door, Delamenko listens. He can't hear a thing. He puts the key in the lock and silently opens the door.

Still nothing.

He racks the slide on the Remington and steps into 205.

CHAPTER 47

A FULLY DRESSED THURSTON rolls out of bed, grabs the knife on the bedside table and comes up in an attack posture.

The room's empty.

He remains completely still. He didn't imagine the ratchet noise. That wasn't part of the dream. He listens intently, sure now his instincts to spend the night across the corridor in the empty 207 were correct.

Thurston hears some soft rustling coming from the corridor and his mind fills in the blanks – three guys, moving quietly.

He pads across to the dresser and picks up the nail gun before crossing towards the door. He looks through the spyhole. Standing outside is a big man carrying an unconscious Terri Greening over his shoulder.

Thurston pads quickly back to the dresser and picks up the crossbow. He loads a bolt into it, and silently turns the handle on the door. The big guy swivels towards 207 and Thurston puts the bolt straight through his eye.

Before he's hit the hotel carpet, Thurston moves into 205 as one of the men unloads three quick rounds into an empty bed. Thurston sees the other turn and bring up his SIG Sauer and drills a two-inch nail into his forehead. He falls forward and slams into the floor, causing his partner to swing the Remington towards Thurston. As the Remington starts *whump*ing Thurston presses the trigger on the nail gun and fires blindly. He hears a grunt as a spray of two-inch nails rips into the assailant's chest.

Behind him, Thurston hears noises as the few guests at the motel begin to stir.

Bleeding heavily, the Remington lying at his feet, the man staggers towards the window and slides back the door to the balcony. Thurston runs forward and kicks him straight over the edge of the balcony rail.

Back in the room, Thurston drops the nail gun and scoops up the Remington and the SIG Sauer before moving into the corridor. A woman in a bathrobe peers out at him through a crack in her door.

'Call the police!' says Thurston. She disappears.

Somebody else appears at the end of the corridor. 'Get back!' shouts Thurston and the guy vanishes.

Thurston looks down and turns Terri over. She's taken a shot to the side of the face – one of the strays from the Remington.

'Shit,' says Thurston and lowers Terri to the carpet.

He runs into 207, collects what little he has and goes back into 205. He closes the door and moves to the balcony. There's no sign of the man on the ground below, but a thick trail of blood leads across the parking lot. Thurston jumps and hits the snow hard. Without looking back he follows the blood trail around a corner.

The bleeding man is slumped on his back in the snow. He makes small gurgling sounds and his eyes are wide.

Thurston takes a step forward and puts a single round into his head, not sure if he's doing it through kindness or hate.

The Jeep is only five metres away.

Thurston stows the guns and crossbow in the passenger footwell and opens the driver's door. He pauses on the threshold before stepping back and returning to the dead man. Taking care not to step in the blood, he drags the body towards the Jeep and bundles him up and over the tailgate.

He's going to send Miller a reply.

CHAPTER 48

MILLER'S PHONE VIBRATES AROUND five in the morning.

He's awake already, wired from too much coke, looking at his laptop. Mercy's asleep, her bruised back turned to Miller. He was rough with her earlier, maybe got carried away, but she seems fine now. They're resilient at that age, Miller has found. He glances at the screen expecting to see Viktor's number.

Instead, it's Riggs.

'OK,' says Miller when he answers.

'I don't know what was supposed to happen down here, Nate, but it sure don't look like it worked out.' Riggs is whispering and Miller can hear talking in the background. 'Wait a minute.'

Miller hears Riggs' muffled voice talking to someone else and then he's back.

'We got three dead. Two I think you might know. Foreigners.'

'Easy,' says Miller, reminding Riggs to be careful. No names.

'Yeah, OK,' says Riggs. 'The woman? Y'know? Terri? She got half her face blown off. They think it was accidental, like.'

'They?'

'Well, here's the thing of it. There's state cops here. Someone at the motel is an off-duty cop. Up here banging his girlfriend. Y'know, somewheres nice and quiet.' Riggs pauses. 'Anyway, this guy, Slater, works robbery-homicide out of Boston Southside and recognised one of the, uh, foreigners. Called his boss and next thing you know we're knee-deep in city badges.'

'Isn't this your town?'

'I tried that,' says Riggs, 'and they said all the right things and so forth – don't wanna step on your toes, jurisdiction blah blah. But bottom line? They ain't shiftin'. They're gonna be doing some digging so I hope the trail don't follow back to—'

'Shut the fuck up!' barks Miller. 'There's nothing traceable. Quit panicking and let them take it back to Boston. A few days and they'll be chasing . . . the visitor. And if that doesn't happen we got some pull down there as insurance.'

'Listen,' says Riggs after a while. 'There's more. We have one big guy with a crossbow bolt through his eye.'

'OK,' says Miller, thinking, *Crossbow?*

'And a smaller dude dead in the bedroom.' Riggs pauses. 'He was shot with a nail gun.'

'Christ Almighty,' says Miller.

'And the last guy? The other guy from Boston?' says Riggs. 'Looks like our "visitor" took him. We got a blood trail leading across the parking lot and a wit who says she saw a body getting bundled into the back of a car. Said it sort of looked like he was – and I'm quoting here – like he was "taking a trophy".'

'A trophy? What the fuck?'

'All I'm doing is passing it along.' Riggs hesitates. 'I don't think this guy is going to be leaving town. I know you guys are, y'know, *capable* and all, but I'd still be careful up there. I think he's coming for you. I think you pissed him off."

Miller hangs up and looks at his reflection staring back at him from the black window.

A *trophy*?

CHAPTER 49

THERE'S A STORM COMING – a bigger one.

Miller can see it in the sky and feel it in his gut. A kind of steel creeps into the already freezing air. The fog lifts slowly to reveal ugly slabs of black cloud crawling across the ridge from the west, like a sheet being drawn over a body in the morgue.

He gets his main guys together in the kitchen at the main house – the Axe, Donno, Carver and Tannhauser – and brings them up to speed on Delamenko's clusterfuck in East Talbot.

'Fuckin' Russians,' says the Axe. 'We shouldn'ta brung them in, Nate.'

'Noted, genius,' says Miller. He holds his hands up. 'I admit it, I fucked up. Should've kept this in-house, like. So we won't say no more about it, OK? Here's what's going to happen. If this guy comes near this place I want him killed. Nothing fancy, just shoot the mother-fucker. I underestimated him. That's not going to happen again. Donno, roust a few of your crew up outta their La-Z-Boys, OK? Get 'em out here now. Same with you, Carver, Tann. All hands on deck. We—'

The kitchen door opens and one of Tannhauser's crew comes in.

Seeing Miller's face, he holds up his hands in apology. 'Sorry, Mr Miller, but, but . . .'

Tannhauser slams a palm on the table. 'Spit it out, Stevie, fer Chrissakes!'

Stevie points to the door. 'You got to see this.'

CHAPTER 50

'**WHAT ARE WE LOOKING** at?' says Miller.

He is standing in the middle of a group of men gathered round a pine tree which has a tarpaulin wrapped around its base.

One of his crew unties a couple of ropes and pulls the tarp free.

Miller coughs and takes a step back. He spits into the snow. 'Holy fuck.'

Viktor Delamenko has been crucified. There's no other word for it. His back lies against the trunk of the giant pine, each hand nailed to a branch on either side. He is naked and a trail of red spots can be clearly seen arcing across his chest. Here and there the light glints on a nail head standing clear of his flesh. He's been shot once in the head through his eye.

'Jesus Christ,' whispers someone behind Miller, and he whips round to see if it's a joke but the guy realises what he's said and holds up a hand.

'How long's he been here?' says Miller.

They are at the junction off the highway that leads to the compound.

Tannhauser's guy, the one who brought the news, steps forward.

'Micky saw him about thirty minutes ago on his way in.' Tannhauser's guy breaks off to point to a guy in his crew. 'Micky figured he'd best cover him up – case anyone spotted him, like.'

'Yeah, good,' says Miller. He turns away from Delamenko. 'Get him down. Get rid of him somewhere far away. He's never been here.'

Tannhauser nods. Micky steps forward with a claw hammer and starts digging the nails out of Delamenko's hands. Miller watches for a few seconds then walks towards his truck. He's at the door when he hears a shout. He turns to see Tannhauser looking closely at something on the trunk of the pine.

'Hey, Nate,' says Tannhauser. 'Check this out.'

Miller steps over Delamenko's body and sees the word 'CHENOO' has been carved into the wood. Blood from Delamenko's wounds has seeped into the grooves.

'Chenoo. What the fuck does that mean?'

Tannhauser shrugs. He turns to the group. 'Anyone?'

One of Carver's boys gets out his phone.

'You fuckin' googling this?' says Miller.

The guy looks at Miller and hesitates. 'Uh, yeah.'

'Good idea,' growls Miller. 'How come none of the rest of you dumb shits thoughta that?'

He's not expecting an answer and none comes.

'It's, uh, Indian,' says the guy looking at his phone. 'Like Red Indian. Native American.'

'What's it mean?' says Miller.

The guy looks up. 'Says here the Chenoo is a human whose heart's been turned into ice. Chenoos are cannibals from the north. Once someone's become, uh, a Chenoo, the only escape is death.'

'Fuckin' crock,' says Miller. He points into the forest. 'Carver, get our four best hunters ready and bazookered up. Huntin' season is officially open. First man to bag this fuckin' "Chenoo" gets a fifty-grand finder's fee. I want this bastard gutted and hung up to rot out here.'

Miller walks back to his truck with Anders. They get in and spin round towards the compound. As soon as he's out of sight of the men, Miller punches the dash hard six times. When he's done he stops, breathing heavily. He glances in his rear-view and slams on the brakes. He turns in his seat to look over his shoulder at a single word traced into the ice on the rear window of the truck.

Chenoo.

CHAPTER 51

SLITHERING BACK INTO HIS position in the snow-covered trees across the highway, Thurston picks up his binoculars to see the guy in front of the dead man looking at his phone. Thurston knows the dude is looking up the word 'Chenoo', exactly like Thurston did earlier.

Thurston knows exactly zip about Native American myths but wanted something spooky-sounding to unsettle Miller's crew. Writing the word on Miller's truck was showy – and risky – but Thurston doesn't care. It was worth it just to think about Miller's face.

Thurston could have taken Nate Miller out with the Remington he picked up in the motel – shit, at this distance he'd fancy his chances of hitting him with the crossbow. But after seeing Terri lying dead in the corridor Thurston's coming at this thing with a new intensity. He's already in the frame for the murders of Sofi and Barb back in London so he's pretty sure he's going to be targeted for the deaths at the Top o' the Lake Motel last night. Which means Cody Thurston is no longer content to kill Nate Miller.

Thurston's going to bring it all down.

CHAPTER 52

IN THE AFTERNOON, THURSTON contents himself with observing. He establishes three vantage points dotted around a sloping ridge. Each of these vantage points is placed high in the branches of a tree and he lays a trail to bring the hunters to him. Nothing too obvious – a broken branch here, some footprints in soft snow there.

It works.

To a point.

After an hour the first of the hunters comes into view. He's moving cautiously on a diagonal across the ridge. If Thurston wasn't being extremely vigilant he'd never have spotted him.

Thurston slides the crossbow into position and tracks the hunter's cautious path, waiting for the moment. He sees a patch of open ground between two trees. *There.*

He waits.

As the hunter gets to the open ground he stops, just as Thurston expects. The guy must know this section might leave him temporarily exposed. What he *should* do is work his way back down the ridge and then edge back up through the tree cover some eighty yards away.

He doesn't.

Thurston's finger tightens on the crossbow trigger and he gets ready to put a bolt in the guy's head the second he appears in the open.

Any second now . . .

Thurston stops.

From everything he's seen, this guy is good. So why is he exposing his position? Why is he taking the risk?

Suddenly Thurston realises what's happening. This guy is bait. They are waiting for Thurston to reveal *his* position. The hunter becomes the hunted.

Smart move, thinks Thurston.

He leans back against the trunk of the tree and waits.

Snow is falling heavily now, drifting down from the steel sky in fat flakes. Inside the forest, the snow-padded silence becomes tangible, the forest a white cathedral. Any noise here will sound like a thunderclap.

So Thurston waits some more.

The temperature keeps falling and he's glad of the extra precautions he's taken with his clothing. He's guessing the hunters, though well equipped, won't have prepared as thoroughly as he has. They are local. They know there are warm beds and food no more than an hour from here on foot. They won't be willing to wait it out as long.

Thurston's betting his life on it.

CHAPTER 53

IT TAKES ALMOST FORTY minutes.

And then Thurston hears the soft crack of a twig underfoot coming from his left, and much closer than he imagined. He swivels his eyes and catches a trace of white vapour rising from a low snow bank about thirty yards behind his position.

These guys have been closing in. He was right to wait. A shot when he saw the first hunter would have resulted in him being trapped. All they'd have to have done was wait it out or shoot him straight out of the tree.

Carefully Thurston takes his cell phone from his pocket and presses a single digit he keyed earlier.

Some hundred metres to his south comes the incongruous muffled sound of a ringtone: a cell placed in the crook of a tree and wrapped inside a woolly hat.

Immediately the hunters move towards the sound. They move more quickly than is advisable, keen to track the ringtone before it gives out. As they edge away from his position, Thurston silently drops to the forest floor.

CHAPTER 54

'SON OF A BITCH.'

Kane, the first of the hunters to get to the phone, holds it up as Palmer and Schmidt arrive.

Palmer grabs Kane's sleeve and pulls him low to the ground. 'Jesus, man!' he hisses. 'Why the fuck you think the phone's there? You want to get us killed?'

Kane's experienced enough to know he's fucked up. A pro, he doesn't get into a slanging match with Palmer. The guy's right. Thurston's drawn them out. They're exposed. The three of them crawl to the bole of a big pine with two protruding protective branches. From here there is only one firing line. Unless Thurston's dead ahead, this will work as protection.

'Where's O'Hara?' says Palmer.

CHAPTER 55

DANNY O'HARA'S AN ARIZONA boy.

He cops plenty of flack on that, mainly about how he can't handle the cold up here. Guys handing him sun lotion, that kind of shit.

But O'Hara was raised in northern Arizona, up in Williams where it gets plenty cold in winter. And he's more cautious than the locals. You don't get to survive six tours of duty in some of the most fucked-up places on the planet without learning a thing or two. The others on this hunt are pros but they've let themselves get caught up in the chase. As soon as the phone rang they were off like dogs catching the scent. O'Hara too, at first, before he stopped and thought some.

This was a trap. This Thurston guy? From what O'Hara has seen, he's solid. Dangerous.

When the phone stops ringing, O'Hara wonders if the others are already dead. He listens intently, straining, but Danny O'Hara hears nothing, not even the sound of Cody Thurston reaching round and cutting his throat in one swift, silent movement.

CHAPTER 56

PALMER SWITCHES TO NIGHT vision goggles as darkness closes in. It turns the snow-covered forest a ghostly, milky green. Fifty yards to Palmer's left, Kane does likewise. Fifty back, Schmidt is bringing up point, the three hunters making an open-faced triangle. They move slowly, deliberately. The phone thing has rattled them, exposed them, but that's forgotten now.

The key for the hunters is to use their local knowledge against Thurston. With the storm worsening there are only so many places he can go. A steep ravine lies to the east. In these conditions it is impassable. To the west is a scrabble of mud and weeds: a flatland area which runs about two miles from the fire trail to Lake Carlson. Even in winter it is not possible to cross.

The phone may have been a plan to draw out the hunters but – from the information they have – Thurston has made an error, trapping himself in a relatively narrow corridor leading back towards White Nation and Lake Carlson. This formation is a net in which to catch Thurston.

After ten minutes, Palmer passes a fallen pine that could make a likely spot for Thurston to mount an attack. He approaches cautiously and sees O'Hara sprawled face down in the snow, the blood spray from his cut throat showing almost black in the night vision goggles. Too late, he realises his mistake.

CHAPTER 57

IN THE SECOND OR two it takes for the man to register his dead comrade, Thurston pulls back the white waterproof under which he's been waiting and puts a crossbow bolt into the back of his head. The hunter slumps forward and lands arched across the fallen pine.

Thurston doesn't wait. Sliding his night vision goggles onto his forehead he turns and, moving quickly, crosses a stand of trees to emerge on the other side of the hunters' 'triangle'. The hunter sees Thurston and raises his rifle.

Thurston flicks on his Maglite torch, blinding the man as he gets off a round. Thurston hears the bullet smack into the tree less than six inches to his left.

The blinded hunter fires wildly as Thurston sprints forward and stabs him in the chest. He shouts something and Thurston hits the ground while the fourth man sets up a hail of shots that cut the blinded hunter almost in two. Blood spurts across the snow as Thurston burrows deep into a drift banked against the base of a big pine. Although not hit, he screams convincingly and pulls on his night vision goggles.

Thurston knows this last guy won't be able to tell if either of the bodies sprawled in the snow are his fellow hunters. Hidden in the drift, Thurston bides his time and then, as number four moves forward fractionally, blows his face off with one round from the Remington.

Thurston emerges from the snowdrift and gets to work.

CHAPTER 58

MORNING CRAWLS ROUND IN the shape of a flat blue-grey light seeping into Isle de Rousse.

At the Talbot Chemical Feed gatehouse, the double-duty security detail has been on full alert all night. The four men have heard the gunfire coming from the forest but Miller's given them instructions to stay put unless advised otherwise.

At five to seven there's enough light for Bridges, the oldest man on duty, to peer through the gatehouse window and see a Jeep parked at the edge of the road where it comes out of the forest.

'Call Miller,' he says. 'Tell him we got sump'n down at the gate.' He picks up his assault rifle and puts on his hat. He motions to another guard, Foley. 'Come with me.'

The wind has picked up and as Bridges and Foley exit the gatehouse a blast of icy air threatens to rip the door off its hinges.

'Let's go,' says Bridges. Foley's moving but doesn't look exactly enthusiastic about the prospect of leaving the gatehouse.

Battling the wind, Bridges and Foley approach the Jeep, their boots squeaking on the new snow. There's something on the hood of the Jeep but with all the snow and wind it's hard to see until they are ten feet away.

'Jesus Christ!' says Foley and pukes.

The windscreen of the Jeep has 'Chenoo' scrawled across it in blood. Lashed to the hood like four hunting trophies are the naked bodies of Kane, Schmidt, Palmer and O'Hara. All of them have had their hearts cut out.

CHAPTER 59

THURSTON'S NO MACHINE.

Exhausted, freezing and hungry, he crawls inside the refuge he prepared yesterday inside the dry 'cave' formed by three fallen trees. A thick layer of smaller branches forms a roof fixed in place now by a carpet of snow. Thurston has sealed every draught with more packed snow and put a double-layered thermal mat on the floor.

He takes off his blood-spattered outer layers and puts on a clean and dry woolly hat. He takes off his boots and carefully wraps them in a protective plastic sheet. He crawls inside a military-grade cold-weather sleeping bag. Sitting up with his back against one of the walls of his refuge, he cracks the foil seal on a self-heating pack of stew and opens a Thermos of hot tea.

Thurston works his way through both before lying down, closing his eyes and falling almost instantly into a bottomless sleep filled with demons.

CHAPTER 60

ANY ICE STORM IS bad news. The one whipping down from Canada and slamming into northern Vermont this morning is a flat-out stone-cold bitch.

The gently drifting snow turns to super-cooled rain and freezes on impact. Within minutes every available surface is covered with a rapidly thickening layer of hard glaze ice as the wind picks up. Power lines bow under the weight, roads become impassable, water pipes freeze solid, vehicles not under cover become glued fast to the ground, their locking systems iced and fuel lines as brittle as an old man's arteries.

By midday, East Talbot is effectively cut off from the rest of the world.

At Isle de Rousse, news about the four dead hunters with the missing hearts spreads through the compound like a virus. With the road now an ice rink, eight men take off on foot within an hour of the news breaking and Miller suspects a few more of the weaker-minded ones are thinking about it. The girls at the compound also hear the rumours but Miller doesn't give a shit if they run. Let the dumb sluts freeze out there. Not one of them would last ten minutes. He's already had to punish Mercy for talking back to him.

No, what's done is done. The hunters on the hood of the Jeep and all that 'Chenoo' bullshit tell Miller one thing: the Australian's declared war. Spooking the men at the compound is smart and a tiny part of Miller grudgingly congratulates his enemy. *First create fear.* Isn't that what some Chink warlord said? But Miller doesn't want any more defections, so he gets the Jeep and the bodies towed out to the old quarry and burned to ash. He has no thoughts on the dead men: just like Viktor and his boys, they fucked up and paid the price.

With the Jeep and the hunters out of the way, Miller concentrates on making the compound an impenetrable fortress. He divides the crews up between Donno and Carver, and lets them sort out rotational patrols, lines of fire and the like. If Thurston's going to come to him then let's see what he's got. Even with the defections, Miller's got better than thirty hard-core guys left with an arsenal that'd make a general's mouth water. They have abundant generator power, a ton of supplies, more drugs than a Colombian cartel, plenty of women . . . all while that Australian bastard's out there freezing his nuts off.

Hell, this might even be fun.

CHAPTER 61

THURSTON CAREFULLY OPENS ONE eye and then the other.

It's more difficult than it sounds – mainly because his eyelids have iced up while he's been sleeping. Although the temperature inside the thermal sleeping bag is pretty good, inside the forest shelter, it has to be said, things are a little on the fresh side.

He wriggles a hand up and rubs ice crystals from his eyes. He checks the illuminated dial of his watch: almost three in the afternoon. Without looking outside he knows something is different. The forest is creaking.

Thurston wriggles to the entrance of his shelter and digs a hole in the protective packed ice. He pushes his head through and sees a changed landscape. Every branch of every tree groans under the weight of glaze ice, the lowest limbs connected to the snowbound forest floor by thick icicles. Thurston realises he's slept through the arrival of an ice storm.

He replaces the snow in the entrance and frees up his arms. He prepares more food and, leaning back against one of the fallen trees, considers his next move. He eyes his backpack and makes a mental list of his armoury. It doesn't fill him with optimism. Thurston's good but he's not Superman. Even if the little show he put on with the Jeep worked, he doesn't think many of the men at the compound will have been spooked enough to leave. He's hopelessly outgunned and, even if they don't try to find him, he won't last too long out here. All Miller has to do is wait it out.

Which means Thurston's got to even up the odds. He thinks back to previous situations and comes up with one word.

Lasqa.

CHAPTER 62

EVERY MAN'S GOT A breaking point. For Cody Thurston it came on 16 June 2007 in Lasqa, Orūzgān Province, southern Afghanistan.

Along with neighbouring Helmand and Kandahar, Orūzgān stood right at the beating black heart of the Taliban.

Bandit country.

Thurston's unit was there under Dutch command as part of the International Security Assistance Force during the battle for Lasqa, a town of some five thousand war-weary souls. The Taliban, seeing Lasqa as a key tactical access point, had taken control of the town in brutal fashion, commandeering civilian homes and farms and exacting brutal vengeance on anyone who resisted. The police commander of the Tander Station was forced to watch his wife's hands being cut off before he was then beheaded. Civilians were given weapons and told by the Taliban: fight with us or be executed.

Thurston's team were instructed to establish a checkpoint a kilo-metre from town and not to engage. Radio chatter soon told the Australians that the Dutch and Afghani troops inside the town were in a dogfight.

'This is fucked,' said Dobbs, Thurston's unit's comms officer. Dobbs was exchanging intel with an interpreter with the Dutch forward force. 'They want us in. It's a bloodbath and we're out here checking licence plates.'

Thurston said nothing. What was there to say? Dobbs was right: this was another fucked situation in a fucked-up place.

Later, the unit heard the Taliban had begun using a school as an ammo dump with the kids still inside so the Dutch and the Afghanis couldn't call in air strikes. In the school, the Taliban beheaded children who attempted to escape as a lesson to the others. On his break, back in the Hummer, Thurston listened to the children's screams for longer than he could stand.

He checked his ammunition and left the Hummer, heading for the small rise that doubled as a field latrine before he cut back north towards the town. As he saw things, something needed to be done. A career soldier to his fingertips, Thurston simply could not sit back and wait as children were slaughtered. He knew that every step he took towards the school was a step away from his life as a soldier. There'd be no way back after this, even if he survived.

Thurston came across a marketplace some three hundred yards from the school where eight Toyota pickup trucks were hidden under cover of the dilapidated stalls. He noted only two guards, one on either side, and he killed both by slitting their throats. He opened the gas tanks of all the vehicles and set them on fire.

He ran back to the school and waited. Less than a minute went by before ten or so men exited. Thurston found a side window and slipped inside. In the main hall were four Taliban fighters at the windows with two or three more standing at the entrance to a back room. Eighty or so children sat in a tight knot in the centre, some of them sobbing. On the fringes of the hall were the discarded bodies of eight or nine executed children. Blood spattered the walls.

Thurston opened fire and killed every man standing.

He shouted and pointed at the door and the children ran without speaking. As they dispersed into the night to find whatever safety they could, Thurston took a grenade and lobbed it into a back room stacked with ammunition cases and weapons.

He ran.

Fifteen minutes later he was back at the checkpoint and his military career was over.

CHAPTER 63

DONNO-JAY DONOFRIO, ONE of Miller's two remaining lieutenants – is in a room in a small office block tacked onto the rear of the main house. This office is the security hub at the compound and is where the CCTV monitors are housed. Half of Donofrio's crew of twelve are actively patrolling the inner perimeter while the others rest. Donofrio is fighting a losing battle with the ice to maintain the security cameras. The storm has already knocked out more than a third and others are falling by the minute. He watches the screens go blank.

'Shit.' He picks up his radio and updates Carver. Carver's in control of the area around the three sheds containing the fermentation tanks that combine the dextrose and benzaldehyde into pseudoephedrine. 'If he comes in to you I can't give you a heads-up,' says Donofrio. 'We're blind down here.'

'If he's coming in through this shit, I'm a Chinaman,' says Carver. 'This storm's kicking up a coupla notches out here.'

Carver pockets his radio and turns the corner of shed 1 into the teeth of the wind. 'Jesus H. Christ,' he mutters as ice rattles into his face. He tightens his goggles and the hood of his parka.

Up ahead he sees two of his crew on the facing corner. Carver looks out at the ice-bound forest beyond the fermentation sheds and wonders if the Australian can possibly still be alive.

CHAPTER 64

THURSTON, WEARING LAYER UPON layer of high-quality thermal protection, huddles in the lee of a big pine and watches the guy near the closest shed put the radio back in his pocket.

Thurston notes a fence post by the man with the radio that houses a security camera. The camera itself is covered in glaze ice and Thurston is betting most, if not all, of the surveillance cameras protecting the compound are out of action.

Thurston steps out of his cover and walks towards the fence. Wearing white and in near-white-out conditions, he is a ghost.

A heavily armed and well-trained ghost.

By the time he's reached the fence, Thurston is less than twenty yards from the corner of the shed. He's watched the patrols enough to know two men are working each section, the first man some ten yards in front of the other.

Which means that the corner of the shed is an opportunity. Thurston puts a bolt into the crossbow and readies the second.

He waits, forcing himself to concentrate. When the first guy comes round he'll only get a few seconds.

After a couple of minutes, the first sentry comes into view. Thurston lets him come round the corner and puts a bolt into his chest. The guy slumps to the snow. Thurston pulls back the bow string and slots in the second bolt. As he's coming up the second sentry comes into view, sees the body on the snow and begins to lift his weapon.

Thurston shoots him in the head with the second bolt. The entire exchange has taken place in complete silence.

Thurston runs back to the forest and prises a fallen log out of the snow. He hauls it back to the fence and throws it against the wire. As he suspected, the fence is no longer electrified. With the power at the compound probably now on a generator there's not enough juice in the system to run what they need and keep the fence on. Thurston pulls out a pair of wire cutters and cuts a gap in the fence. He pushes through and runs to the corner of shed 1. From here he can see sheds 2 and 3 looking like blurred paper cut-outs through the ice storm. The wind is now coming in almost horizontally. Thurston battles his way across the open space to shed 2. When the sentries come round he kills them both – the first with the crossbow, the second with his hunting knife. At shed 3 he repeats the routine.

According to his calculations there's still one guy remaining: the guy with the radio. Thurston has him pegged as the boss of this crew but there's no way of telling where he is now. Thurston can't wait. He finds a door leading into shed 3 and slides it back on its track.

Inside, Thurston pushes back his goggles and takes a breath. At first he thinks there is someone moving inside the vast space but realises it is the storm lashing the tin walls.

Six gleaming steel vats stand in a row down the centre of the shed. A low electric hum sits under the sound of the wind.

Thurston takes off his backpack, from which he takes three aerosols of hairspray and a small tin of lighter fluid. He places an aerosol each under three of the vats and opens the valves. An acrid stench begins to fill the shed. Thurston squirts the lighter fluid around the base of the aerosols. He flicks a lighter and moves down the shed, setting a flame to the lighter fluid.

Thurston exits the shed and runs straight into the guard.

CHAPTER 65

'WE GOT A RUNNER,' says the Axe.

Miller gets up off his chair and joins Axel Anders at the window overlooking the lake.

One of the compound girls, wearing jeans and a parka, is slipping and sliding across the frozen lake, moving away from the house.

'That dumb bitch ain't gonna make it,' says Miller.

'You want me to fetch her back?'

Miller shakes his head. 'Fuck her.'

He and Anders watch the girl get swallowed by the whiteness. It's a two-hour hike across to East Talbot. In this storm, dressed like she is, the girl will be dead within the hour.

'We shouldn't be sitting back and waiting,' says Anders. The big man lumbers across to the bar and pours out a bourbon.

Miller taps out a line of coke on the marble and hoovers it up greedily. He's been getting increasingly wired with each passing hour of inactivity.

'I don't like it any more than you, Axe,' he says. 'But we—'

Miller stops mid-sentence as a gunshot sounds from somewhere outside. He looks towards Anders, and then three explosions come in quick succession, sending a shock wave rippling across the compound.

'I guess he's here,' growls Anders. He smiles and reaches for his gun. 'Rock and roll!'

'You dumb shit,' snarls Miller. 'That bastard's blown the sheds!'

CHAPTER 66

FOR A BIG GUY, the guard moves quick. Almost too quick.

The muzzle of his assault rifle cuts up towards Thurston in a vicious arc that would have broken Thurston's jaw if he hadn't managed to step inside the blow and drive the heel of his hand hard into the man's nose.

Blood flashes through the air and he howls like a bastard. Thurston snaps the rifle out of the man's hands but it slips from his grasp and skitters across the ice, out of reach.

Thurston takes a step back to give himself room and reaches for his knife. As his fingers close round the handle, the guard recovers his senses enough to come roaring back at Thurston like a grizzly with its tail on fire. He traps Thurston's hand inside his parka and wraps a meaty forearm around the Australian's throat. Thurston takes a step backwards that fractionally unbalances his opponent. Using his weight against him, Thurston dips a shoulder and in one fluid twist flips his attacker over.

As the man tumbles through the icy air, a trailing boot catches Thurston a glancing blow on the side of his head. Both men slam to the ice.

The guard is the first one to move.

He rolls over and scrambles for his weapon. His gloved fingers close around the trigger as he sits up to bring the weapon to bear on the still dazed Thurston.

Behind the two men, shed 3 explodes.

The guard, his body forming a barrier between Thurston and the worst of the explosion, is sliced clean in two by a twisted sheet of flaming metal. Thurston feels a flash of searing heat before everything turns black.

CHAPTER 67

AFTER FINDING THE SIX dead from Carver's crew and seeing shed 3 going up in flames, three of Donofrio's crew have had enough. They take off in one of the compound Hummers. With the road to East Talbot impassable, they head across the lake.

Donofrio is making his way across to the two remaining sheds when he sees the tail lights fading into the storm just as Miller and Anders emerge from the main house heading towards what's left of shed 3. Donofrio stops in his tracks.

He's loyal to Miller – he's got a slice of the action and, truth be told, it's been pretty sweet so far – but this situation is way beyond messed up. Miller's been holed up in the house snorting product for what seems like days. He's acting like he's running an army but the fact is his army is now down to less than six. As tight as Miller might be with the local cops, something on this scale will be investigated once the ice storm stops. Unless Miller gets very lucky there'll be Feds crawling all over Isle de Rousse before the weekend.

It's time to call it.

Donofrio gets out his radio and brings his three remaining guys in.

Let Miller and Anders duke it out with whoever this guy is. The Australian might not be this supernatural Chenoo deal but Donofrio knows one thing: he ain't normal.

CHAPTER 68

NICK TERRAVERDI MAKES IT to East Talbot around five. If he wasn't already in Hanover he wouldn't have attempted the journey. As it was he skidded off the road more times than he cares to think about.

Still, he had to come. If this is what he knows it is – that little adventure Cody Thurston told him about back in New York – then he needs to be there to stop this turning into another fucking Waco.

In the entrance to the police station Terraverdi finds Bernie Slater, the robbery-homicide guy who called Boston about the three dead bodies at the Top o' the Lake Motel. A friend at Boston who knows the Russians' link to organised crime called the FBI. Since Delamenko and his boys crossed several state lines, this is a Fed case. Terraverdi pulled a couple of favours to be the one assigned.

'So what's the situation?' says Terraverdi after the preliminaries.

Slater's a thirty-year vet. He moves slow but Terraverdi wouldn't like to be on the wrong side of him. Like most state cops he's not given to warmth when it comes to the FBI, but Terraverdi's seen worse.

'I was in the motel,' says Slater. 'With a friend.' He looks at Terraverdi, who says nothing. 'OK, well, like I say, I was there with a friend. Then this shit happened and I come out to see three bodies.

Two in the corridor and one in the bedroom. The woman was shot – something automatic, large calibre. The first guy had a fuckin' crossbow bolt through his fuckin' head . . .'

'Jesus!' says Terraverdi.

'That ain't the kicker. The second guy? The one in 205? He's taken one in the balls and one in the noggin from a nail gun.'

'A nail gun?'

Slater nods. 'Uh-huh.' He glances towards the station office where Riggs is sitting at a desk. 'The asswipe there, Riggs: he's the local sheriff. He told me these guys must have been passing through. Can you believe that shit? Three connected Russians from Southie take a fuckin' winter break up here and wind up dead.'

'Three?'

'Oh,' says Slater, 'I forgot that part. There's a wit who saw a third guy get whacked in the parking lot. From my experience? I'm saying he's Viktor Delamenko. Anyway, this Delamenko was already wounded – I'm guessing nail gun – and jumped outta the bedroom window. Our wit says another guy put one in Viktor's head and took him away in the back of a Jeep. You ever heard anything like that?'

He's about to reply to Slater when a muffled boom echoes across Lake Carlson.

'Christ Almighty!' says Slater. 'What was that?'

Terraverdi sighs.

Thurston, you motherfucker.

CHAPTER 69

THURSTON OPENS HIS EYES and sees nothing except white.

He blinks a few times, raises his head and slowly the world reassembles. Light and sound and smell rush in.

Behind him, shed 3 burns, the flames ripping diagonally away from where he is lying in the snow – a few degrees different and he'd be toast.

Thurston pushes what remains of the guard off him and staggers upright. Thurston's goggles are gone and parts of his weatherproof parka looks as if someone took a cheese-grater to it, but there doesn't appear to be any major physical damage: a cut to his head and a ringing in one ear. Right now, he's more concerned about his weapons.

The Remington is screwed. The same goes for the crossbow, which lies in a tangled mess about three yards away. Thurston finds the guard's weapon but it too is hopelessly damaged.

Thurston starts moving towards the main house as fire takes hold of shed 2. Once that went it became only a matter of time before shed 1 completes the set. Thurston keeps to what cover he can find and makes his way down to the lake shore.

The house looks deserted as he approaches from the lake. Coming up under the extended deck he forces a side window and slips inside. He moves through the house room by room, becoming increasingly confident the place is deserted. It looks as though the tactic he used back in Afghanistan has worked, driving out the enemy from their stronghold. If it wasn't for running slap into the guard he'd be picking off Miller and the Axe right now. Thurston takes a large knife from the kitchen and puts it in his pocket; it's not much but it'll have to do.

In the basement, Thurston comes across a metal door that looks like somewhere Miller might keep weapons. He slowly turns the lock and pushes the door open.

It's not an armoury. It's a dungeon.

The walls are painted black with a low red vinyl couch running along one side of the room. Various sadomasochistic items are dotted here and there on the bare concrete floor. A large-screen TV hangs on one wall.

Huddled on the red couch are three teenage girls dressed in skimpy clothes. They look terrified and Thurston can't blame them. He is an apparition from hell. Blood from the cut on his head has run down to form a grisly red mask over one side of his face. His blood- and smoke-scarred parka hangs in tattered strips down his back.

Thurston approaches the girls and bends low. They scrabble back away from him like startled birds as he approaches.

'I'm not here to hurt you,' he whispers, holding his hands up. 'But you have to listen to me if you want to get out of here alive, OK?' There's no response but Thurston carries on. 'Are there any more of you in the house?'

They look at each other and then the youngest of them nods. 'Mercy's somewhere upstairs,' she says.

'Mercy?'

'She's his favourite,' says another girl.

'Miller's?'

'Uh-huh. Yeah. But she done something wrong. Spoke back to him or sump'n, I dunno. Nate don't like anyone speakin' back to him. He's got her up in punishment.'

Thurston frowns. 'Punishment?'

The girl raises her eyes to the ceiling. 'In the storeroom.'

Thurston stands. 'I'm going to get Mercy, OK? You stay here until I come back. I'm going to get you out of here.'

As he leaves the dungeon Thurston looks back. None of the girls look as if they believe him.

CHAPTER 70

THE PSEUDOEPHEDRINE IN THE three sheds would be worth something north of two hundred million dollars once it's channelled into Europe via Reykjavik. With shed 3 gone already, Miller's looking at being wiped out if the others follow.

Which they do.

Miller and Anders are less than fifty yards from shed 2 when it blows. The shock wave knocks them flat on their asses, and before they can get to their feet shed 1 erupts, sending a second monstrous fireball up into the steely sky. The air fills with the stench of burning chemicals as glowing embers are whipped away on the wind, mingling with the snow and ice.

Miller staggers to his feet and, peering through the storm, contemplates the ruins of his empire. Next to him, Anders, brushing splinters of metal from his sleeve, stays silent.

Miller's head sinks to his chest and remains there for a while. When it comes up again his eyes glow with a dull red hate.

'Get everyone together,' he says, the words rumbling like thunder. 'I'm going to skin this motherfucker.'

'There ain't no one, Nate.' Anders turns his face away from the wind. 'They've gone, man. Every last one of 'em.'

Miller turns to face the giant. 'And you? You thinking of lightin' out too like all the other pussies? Because if you are, then be my guest.'

Anders' face clouds. He steps closer to Miller and jabs a finger in his boss's chest. 'I'm still here, aren't I?' he growls. 'And don't forget, *Nate*, I was in for ten per cent of the product we just watched go up in smoke. You ain't the only one who's suffering here.'

Miller holds up a placatory hand. 'Yeah, OK, I know.' He turns away from Anders and stalks back towards the main house. 'Let's go kill that fuckin' Australian.'

CHAPTER 71

THURSTON PAUSES ON THE first-floor landing. At first, all he can hear is the muffled rattle of ice hitting the walls of the property. The sound rises and falls with the wind.

But then he picks up another noise he can't quite identify. He moves towards a door at the end of a corridor and the sound crystallises into something human. The sound of crying.

Thurston opens the door cautiously.

The room is some kind of storage space, one wall lined with metal shelving stacked high with cardboard boxes, cleaning products and household items. It's cold.

Chained to a radiator against one wall is a young girl wearing nothing but a bra and the padlocked dog collar connecting one end of her chain to the radiator. Bruises stand out angrily on her pale skin and one of her eyes is caked in dried blood. She shivers uncontrollably, both knees drawn high, arms wrapped tightly round her shins.

At the sight of Thurston she shrinks back against the radiator. Thurston takes off his tattered parka and wraps it round her.

'I'll try and get you out of here, Mercy,' he says. He turns his attention to the collar but the thing is solid.

'You know where the key is?' he asks.

Mercy shakes her head. She points a trembling finger at the door.

'Miller's got it?'

She nods, her eyes widening at the name.

'Does he have weapons in the house?' says Thurston.

Before the girl can say anything, from downstairs comes the sound of a door opening and closing. Mercy flashes a look of pure terror in Thurston's direction.

Someone's in the house.

He signals for the girl to stay quiet and moves towards the door.

Mercy has a strange look on her face that Thurston can't figure out. Then, too late, he realises what she's doing: making a calculation about her survival chances. A calculation coming down heavily on the side of Nate Miller.

'Here!' she screams. 'Up here! He's here!'

Thurston can't blame her. She's a child. Besides, with things as they are, Miller might *be* the kid's best option. Unarmed and trapped upstairs, his own chances don't look too good right now.

Leaving Mercy screaming, Thurston moves into the hallway and sprints towards the stairs. Looking over the landing rail he sees Miller coming up holding a shotgun.

Thurston jerks his head back in the nick of time.

A blast from Miller's gun punches a hole in the ceiling, the round passing so close to Thurston's face he can feel the heat. Thurston runs past the storage room to the window and slides the sash up. He's looking out at a high sloping roof extending out over the deck. Behind him he hears Miller clattering up the stairs.

Thurston launches himself through the window as another shotgun blast shatters the glass. He hits the roof and rolls out of control towards the guttering. He tries to grip something but the glaze ice makes it an impossibility and he skids out into space.

For a split second Thurston hangs in the air and then slams, back first, onto the padded cover of the hot tub six yards below.

It saves his life.

The cover splits and Thurston feels the air pushed out of his lungs as he drops into the water. He pushes up and scrambles over the side as Miller gets a bead on him from the upper window. A blast splinters the edge of the hot tub and Thurston slithers across the iced-up deck, his breath rasping as he desperately tries to get oxygen back into his lungs.

'He's on the deck!' yells Miller and Thurston glimpses the Axe at the fold-back doors.

The Axe is holding a US Special Ops M4A1 assault rifle. It's a big gun but looks like a toy in the giant's hands. Slung under the barrel is an M203 40mm grenade launcher.

Thurston jumps off the deck as the Axe fires the grenade.

Behind Thurston the hot tub and deck railing disappear and Thurston feels a sharp pain in his thigh. As he slides helplessly down towards the lake he sees a shard of fibreglass has embedded itself in his leg.

After sliding fifty or sixty yards, Thurston hits the lake and skids three yards more before coming to a halt, the blood from his leg wound tracing a smear across the ice.

He staggers to his feet and begins moving as quickly as he can. The Axe reaches the edge of the deck and starts firing. Thurston zigzags as the bullets tear into the thick ice. Now he hears a second blast and realises that Miller has joined the Axe at the deck edge. At this range Thurston knows he's a difficult target and he pushes forward, ignoring the pain. Every yard is a yard closer to safety.

The shooting stops and Thurston glances back to see Miller and the Axe clambering down towards the lake. With eight inches of plastic buried in Thurston's leg, he knows they're going to gain on him once they get onto the lake.

He needs an edge.

CHAPTER 72

'**WE GET HIM ALIVE,**' says Miller. 'I want this bastard to suffer.'

He and Anders are tracking Thurston across the lake. It's not difficult. Thurston's wound is leaving a trail anyone could follow.

'He's heading north,' says Anders. 'Maybe he's planning on getting into the woods.'

'He ain't gonna make it that far,' says Miller and points. About a hundred yards ahead is Thurston, lying on the ice. 'Go get him,' he says. 'Drag him back to the house. Have us a party.'

'My pleasure,' says Anders. He shoulders his rifle and unhooks the axe from the pouch on his belt. 'He might be missing an arm or two.'

'Fine with me, man.' Miller takes out a cigarette and bends away from the wind. 'Just bring him back still breathing. We owe this cocksucker.'

Anders walks towards Thurston, the axe swinging easy at his side.

He's going to enjoy this.

CHAPTER 73

AS THE GIANT MAN approaches, Thurston forces himself to remain still. For this to work the guy has to be close.

Thurston's using an old Spec Ops 'fishing' tactic with himself as bait. He hasn't picked this part of the lake by chance. Less than fifty yards to Thurston's right lies the marshy estuary area that forms one of the northern boundaries to the compound.

The lake ice here is thinner. Much thinner. Thurston has edged as close as he dares to where the thick ice gives way to the thinner skein put in place by the ice storm. Lying on his back, he hears it creaking below him like the deck of an old wooden ship.

The Axe is about twenty yards from Thurston when the ice cracks and a slice of black water opens up behind him like a devil's smile.

He stops and slowly takes his assault rifle off his back and takes aim at Thurston.

The ice suddenly shifts and the big man almost falls. With his arms windmilling as he tries to regain balance, the M4A1 slips from his fingers and disappears into the water. As the ice disintegrates, the giant sprints hard towards the Australian, his axe raised high.

Thurston gets ready.

He's gambled on the Axe's greater weight being enough to break the ice and drop him into the lake.

It isn't working: the Axe is closing in fast.

Behind him, black water cracks open at a frightening rate but the giant is still closing in. Thurston gets to his feet and picks up the knife. With the storm whipping across the lake he balances the blade and waits. He doesn't want this to become a hand-to-hand fight.

When the Axe is less than three yards away, Thurston takes his shot. Bending on one knee, he throws the knife and it hits its target high in the chest.

And does precisely nothing.

The giant brings down the axe in a vicious swing which, if it connected, would have taken Thurston's arm off. Instead, the blade slices through fabric, grazing Thurston's flesh on the way through. Thurston steps in close and grabs the handle of the knife sticking out of the Axe's chest. The man screams but before Thurston can stab him, the ice below their feet shatters into a thousand pieces and both men plunge into the dark water.

The water is impossibly, ridiculously cold: a cold so profound and bone-numbingly shocking in intensity that, for a few seconds, Thurston finds it difficult to think.

The Axe, gripping Thurston's arms tightly, wears an expression of grim satisfaction as the two men sink. There's nothing Thurston can do – no way of getting out of the giant's death hold.

But Thurston has a crucial advantage: not only is he a Special

Forces-trained free diver, and the most stubborn individual in the northern hemisphere, under all this padding he's wearing a nine-millimetre-thick drysuit.

The bald fact is that he can wait this out longer than the stronger man.

Almost thirty seconds elapses before it dawns on the Axe that the passive Thurston seems more comfortable than someone should be in his situation. The realisation hits the giant like a punch in the face. His eyes widen and Thurston sees the first stream of panicked air bubbles escape the big man's nostrils. In an instant, instinct takes over. The Axe releases Thurston and scrambles wildly towards the surface.

Thurston has other ideas.

He reaches out and grabs hold of the giant's ankle.

Now in full-blown panic, the Axe thrashes wildly, arms flailing, vital oxygen bubbling from his lungs, his brain unable to compute what is happening. Gradually his movements slow and then, as the last scrap of oxygen leaves his body, the giant's brain shuts down and his body relaxes as he dies.

Thurston releases him, kicks for the surface and hits the solid ice lying on top of Lake Carlson like a coffin lid.

Shit.

They must have drifted further than Thurston thought. He desperately punches the ice but it's no use. Fighting his own rising panic, he wastes precious seconds trying to find the hole in the ice but comes up short. And then he remembers the knife sticking out of the Axe's chest.

He pushes down hard, the cold sucking feeling from his fingers. He doesn't have much time left. *Tick tock.*

With his heart rate slowing to cryogenic levels and his adrenaline screaming off the charts, Thurston finds the dead man and the knife. As the last of his breath dribbles from his lungs, Thurston hauls the blade free and powers up towards the surface, driving the blade as hard as he can into the underside of the ice.

CHAPTER 74

IF ANYTHING, THE STORM'S getting worse.

Miller retreats further onto solid ice away from the gaping black mouth that swallowed Anders and the Australian. The open water slices across the lake and curves round Miller, preventing him from going in a direct line back to the house.

He's in no real danger – the ice out here is strong enough to take a truck – but it's going to be a long cold walk back, especially if the threatened white-out materialises.

Miller keeps the spot where the two men disappeared in view, but so much time has passed he's sure now both men are dead. Still, he waits longer. There've been too many surprises with this Australian fuck.

Eventually, he shoulders his weapon and, hunching his shoulders into the teeth of the icy wind, begins the walk back to what's left of his compound through the thickening white spindrift.

He has taken only two paces when he hears an odd crunching sound coming from behind him.

He turns to see a knife splinter upwards through the ice.

'What the fuck . . . ?' mutters Miller. He swings his gun back round and squints through the snow.

The arm vanishes and then comes back up again, this time followed by another arm and Thurston's head. Miller starts moving towards him as Thurston hauls himself up and out onto the thicker ice. Shivering violently, he crawls to safety and staggers to his feet just as Miller closes in.

CHAPTER 75

'YOU'RE ONE HARD SON of a bitch to kill, Crocodile Dundee,' says Miller, pointing the ugly snout of his rifle directly at Thurston's head. 'I'll give you that. Now drop the knife, chief, and kick it this way.'

Thurston looks at Miller.

'Don't,' says Miller. 'I know you're thinking about throwing the knife but I have to say you got no—'

Before Miller can react, Thurston throws the knife but it slips from his trembling fingers and skitters harmlessly to Miller's feet.

Miller laughs. 'Fuckin' awesome! Some primo James fuckin' Bond shit right there!' He raises the rifle sight to his eye and takes five or six steps forward. 'I was planning to get you somewhere quiet and go to work on you for a day or two . . . y'know, get some "closure" on this giant clusterfuck. But, shit, it's just getting too goddamn cold so I reckon I'll just blow your cocksuckin' Australian brains out right here.'

'Y-you t-t-talk t-too much,' Thurston manages to say.

'Oh, r-r-really?' says Miller and pulls the trigger.

Nothing happens.

He pulls again . . . and nothing.

Both men realise at the same instant what has happened: the

plunging temperatures out here on Lake Carlson have frozen the mechanism on Miller's rifle.

Thurston starts running at Miller as the American throws his rifle to one side and bends to pick up the knife. Miller comes up with it in his right hand and backs off warily as Thurston approaches, the two men moving in slow circles around one another. The spindrift has now developed into the threatened white-out and Miller and Thurston are the only moving elements in an icy universe. The lake shore vanishes as north, west, south and east become indistinguishable.

'*Star T-Trek*,' says Thurston.

'What?' says Miller.

'*Star Trek*. There's alw-ways a-a scene where K-Kirk battles some fuck-ugly a-alien, y'know? I'm Kirk, b-by th-the way.'

Miller charges, the knife slashing viciously through the air, but this isn't Miller's game. Thurston dances out of his way and smashes an elbow hard into the side of Miller's head as he passes. The American grunts but keeps slashing with the blade. An image of Mercy chained to the radiator flashes into Thurston's mind and he feels a fresh wave of anger surge through his frozen body. He steps in and breaks Miller's right arm with a pile-driving heel stamp. Miller screams and drops the knife as Thurston whips round with a second kick that pops the American's kneecap.

Miller drops to the ice, his right arm hanging at a sickening angle. Thurston hits him hard in the ribs before driving a short jab into Miller's face that puts him on his back. Thurston takes the knife and stands above the beaten man, breathing heavily.

Miller groans and tries to stand but can't. The effort puts pressure on his broken limbs and he screams again. He pukes into the snow and lies back on the ice, grimacing up at Thurston, his teeth ringed with blood.

'You broke my fuckin' arm, man,' Miller spits. 'Why'd you break my fuckin' arm?'

'Lasqa,' says Thurston.

'What? What the fuck is Lasqa?'

'A place in Afghanistan, Miller. Had a lot of little kids there, kids not much younger than the girls you got up in that Nazi sewer of yours. Let's call the arm payback for Lasqa, and the knee for all the shit you did to the girls.'

Thurston steps closer and stands on Miller's nuts. As Miller writhes, Thurston bends close.

'That's for Sofi,' he hisses.

He steps away and in a quick twisting motion breaks Miller's left arm. Miller howls.

'And that's for Barb Connors, you piece of shit.'

Thurston stands over Miller and waits for him to stop sobbing.

'What now, smartass?' Miller coughs. 'You can kill me but sure as shit you'll freeze to death before you make it back to the fuckin' house, genius. So go ahead, fuckin' do it.'

Thurston shakes his head. 'You got it all back to front, Miller. I'm not going to kill you.'

Miller looks puzzled and Thurston smiles.

'I'm going to rob you.'

CHAPTER 76

'MOTHERFUCKER! MOTHER*FUCKER*!' MILLER'S AGONISED screams are muffled by the relentless wind and snow. The blood and snot around his nose begins to freeze solid. His black hair and goatee are fast being covered with a frosting of ice crystals.

Thurston adjusts the zip on the parka he's taken from Miller and settles Miller's goggles across his eyes.

'This is some grade-A gear you got, Miller,' says Thurston. He waggles the fingers of the gloves and looks down at the snow boots. 'Toasty.'

Miller, shivering helplessly on the ice, is naked except for a pair of boxer shorts.

'I'm only leaving those shit-stained drawers on you because I don't want to see your shrivelled little pecker, Miller,' says Thurston. 'That's the kind of shit you can't unsee.'

From somewhere out in the whiteness, sirens wail.

Thurston bends his face close to Miller and drops his voice. 'I guess even out here an explosion that big will have attracted attention. Or maybe one of your loyal little Nazi soldiers blabbed. Or, and this is the option I'm going for, maybe it's my old buddy Nicky Terraverdi at the FBI, coming to make sure your little pet Riggs didn't sweep all this under the carpet. Either way, you are done, Miller. You shouldn't have killed Sofi or Barb.'

Miller's mouth opens but no sound emerges.

Thurston holds his eyes on Miller's. The sirens are closer now. Miller's heart tolls like a funeral bell as snow settles on his skin, his life dissolving into nothing.

Thurston waits until he is sure Miller is dead and then, using the rifle as a lever, stands with some difficulty. He'll have to get the splinter in his leg fixed when he reaches civilisation. There's a medic in Burlington whom Thurston can trust. It'll be the last time Cody Thurston calls in an old favour because Cody Thurston will be left out on Lake Carlson, along with Michael Flanagan, both as dead as Nate Miller.

But there'll be other names, and other towns. The world's a big place with plenty of dark corners and an adaptable guy like him can always find work. There'll be somewhere.

Limping, the Australian walks away from the closing sirens towards the welcoming spindrift whipped up by the ice storm. In ten yards, he's nothing more than a grey silhouette, a ghost.

And then, in ten more, he is gone.

An anonymous caller has promised to set off deadly bombs in Washington, D.C. A cruel hoax or the real deal? By the time Alex Cross and his wife, Bree Stone, uncover the chilling truth, it may already be too late . . .

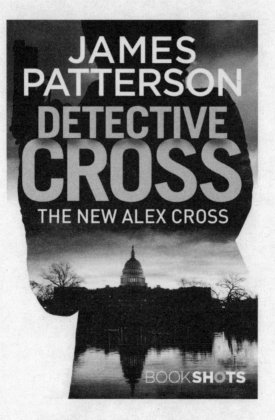

The new Alex Cross thriller. Out now.

BOOK**SHOTS**

BOOKSHOTS

STORIES AT THE SPEED OF LIFE

www.bookshots.com

ALSO BY JAMES PATTERSON

ALEX CROSS NOVELS

Along Came a Spider

Kiss the Girls

Jack and Jill

Cat and Mouse

Pop Goes the Weasel

Roses are Red

Violets are Blue

Four Blind Mice

The Big Bad Wolf

London Bridges

Mary, Mary

Cross

Double Cross

Cross Country

Alex Cross's Trial (*with Richard DiLallo*)

I, Alex Cross

Cross Fire

Kill Alex Cross

Merry Christmas, Alex Cross

Alex Cross, Run

Cross My Heart

Hope to Die

Cross Justice

Cross the Line

THE WOMEN'S MURDER CLUB SERIES

1st to Die

2nd Chance (*with Andrew Gross*)

3rd Degree (*with Andrew Gross*)

4th of July (*with Maxine Paetro*)

The 5th Horseman (*with Maxine Paetro*)

The 6th Target (*with Maxine Paetro*)

7th Heaven (*with Maxine Paetro*)

8th Confession (*with Maxine Paetro*)

9th Judgement (*with Maxine Paetro*)

10th Anniversary (*with Maxine Paetro*)

11th Hour (*with Maxine Paetro*)

12th of Never (*with Maxine Paetro*)

Unlucky 13 (*with Maxine Paetro*)

14th Deadly Sin (*with Maxine Paetro*)

15th Affair (*with Maxine Paetro*)

16th Seduction (*with Maxine Paetro*)

DETECTIVE MICHAEL BENNETT SERIES

Step on a Crack (*with Michael Ledwidge*)

Run for Your Life (*with Michael Ledwidge*)

Worst Case (*with Michael Ledwidge*)

Tick Tock (*with Michael Ledwidge*)

I, Michael Bennett (*with Michael Ledwidge*)

Gone (*with Michael Ledwidge*)

Burn (*with Michael Ledwidge*)

Alert (*with Michael Ledwidge*)

Bullseye (*with Michael Ledwidge*)

Haunted (*with James O. Born*)

PRIVATE NOVELS

Private (*with Maxine Paetro*)

Private London (*with Mark Pearson*)

Private Games (*with Mark Sullivan*)

Private: No. 1 Suspect (*with Maxine Paetro*)

Private Berlin (*with Mark Sullivan*)

Private Down Under (*with Michael White*)

Private L.A. (*with Mark Sullivan*)
Private India (*with Ashwin Sanghi*)
Private Vegas (*with Maxine Paetro*)
Private Sydney (*with Kathryn Fox*)
Private Paris (*with Mark Sullivan*)
The Games (*with Mark Sullivan*)
Private Delhi (*with Ashwin Sanghi*)

NYPD RED SERIES

NYPD Red (*with Marshall Karp*)
NYPD Red 2 (*with Marshall Karp*)
NYPD Red 3 (*with Marshall Karp*)
NYPD Red 4 (*with Marshall Karp*)

DETECTIVE HARRIET BLUE SERIES

Never Never (*with Candice Fox*)
Fifty Fifty (*with Candice Fox*)

STAND-ALONE THRILLERS

Sail (*with Howard Roughan*)
Swimsuit (*with Maxine Paetro*)
Don't Blink (*with Howard Roughan*)
Postcard Killers (*with Liza Marklund*)
Toys (*with Neil McMahon*)
Now You See Her (*with Michael Ledwidge*)
Kill Me If You Can (*with Marshall Karp*)
Guilty Wives (*with David Ellis*)
Zoo (*with Michael Ledwidge*)
Second Honeymoon (*with Howard Roughan*)
Mistress (*with David Ellis*)
Invisible (*with David Ellis*)
The Thomas Berryman Number

Truth or Die (*with Howard Roughan*)
Murder House (*with David Ellis*)
Woman of God (*with Maxine Paetro*)
Hide and Seek
Humans, Bow Down (*with Emily Raymond*)
The Black Book (*with David Ellis*)
Murder Games (*with Howard Roughan*)
Black Market
The Midnight Club
The Store (*with Richard DiLallo*)

BOOKSHOTS

Black & Blue (*with Candice Fox*)
Cross Kill
Private Royals (*with Rees Jones*)
The Trial (*with Maxine Paetro*)
Chase (*with Michael Ledwidge*)
French Kiss (*with Richard DiLallo*)
Killer Chef (*with Jeffrey J. Keyes*)
The Christmas Mystery (*with Richard DiLallo*)
Come and Get Us (*with Shan Serafin*)
Hidden (*with James O. Born*)
Malicious (*with James O. Born*)
French Twist (*with Richard DiLallo*)
The Exile (*with Alison Joseph*)
The End (*with Brendan DuBois*)
After the End (*with Brendan DuBois*)
The Shut-In (*with Duane Swierczynski*)
Private Gold (*with Jassy Mackenzie*)
Detective Cross
The Women's War (*with Shan Serafin*)
Deadly Cargo (*with Will Jordan*)
The Medical Examiner (*with Maxine Paetro*)